OF MICE AND MEN

OF MICE AND MEN

BY

JOHN STEINBECK

WITH AN INTRODUCTION BY

JOSEPH HENRY JACKSON

THE

MODERN LIBRARY

NEW YORK

MODERN LIBRARY EDITION, 1938

Copyright, 1937, by John Steinbeck
Copyright renewed, 1965, by John Steinbeck

Manufactured in the United States of America

INTRODUCTION

By JOSEPH HENRY JACKSON

PUT John Steinbeck on a street corner with three or four other men, talking. Then bring along a panhandler: a workingman down on his luck, or one of the wise boys that know how to pick them, or just a wine-bum. Any of the three will choose Steinbeck every time. The workingman recognizes a fellow worker. The wise boy knows the signs of the man who would rather shell out to a faker than take a chance on turning down one who really needs a handout. The wine-bum, in spite of his fuddlement, instinctively understands that here is kindliness, simplicity, tenderness of heart. And each is right. Steinbeck has worked with his hands early and often, on ranches, with cattle, up in the heights of the California Sierra. Because he has been one of them he can never bring himself to risk letting a workingman go hungry while he has anything in his own pocket. As for his essential gentleness, his sympathy, his ready understanding of any kind of human being, those things are as natural to him as breathing.

Salinas, center of California's lettuce industry and lettuce strikes, and by way of being a meeting place for cattlemen as well as ranchers, lies up near the northern end of the Salinas River Valley, eighty miles south of San Francisco. John Ernest Steinbeck was born in Salinas thirty-five years ago. There is German blood in him, and a large admixture of Irish. Tall—an inch or so over six feet—and massively put together, he suggests the Teuton until you look at this face. Then the inquiring blue eye under its perpetually raised eyebrow flatly contradicts the hint of stolidity in his proportions; it is as Irish as his sense of humor, which is enormous. You could probably go a little fey yourself trying to pin down the curiously Celtic quality in a man so solidly and ruddily German-seeming. That is, you could if he didn't happen to be there to cock an eyebrow at you and stop you with a bunkhouse word. He knows plenty of bunkhouse words. He should, since he has a large acquaintance with bunkhouses and the men who live in them.

His association with bunkhouses and working-men began while he was in school. A lot of boys down in the Valley work while they are getting their education; it's a matter of course with most of them. Young Steinbeck was running cultiva-tors, bucking grain-bags, doing odd jobs around cattle all through his Salinas High School days. Later, when he had learned enough chemistry, he worked for a while in the laboratory of the big Spreckels sugar refinery near by. Once he was a straw-boss on a Valley ranch. Cattle, farm-ing, chemistry, it was all the same to him. Even as a kid he was interested in everything. That characteristic has been enlarged and developed by the years.

INTRODUCTION

He doesn't remember now why he decided to go to college or why, having made up his mind, he chose Stanford. Some of his family had gone to Stanford; perhaps that had something to do with it. At any rate, he went up to Palo Alto, made it plain to the faculty that he had no intention of taking a degree, watched the pained expression on the face of the registrar with some interest, repeated that he wanted to study certain subjects but not others, and, having been accepted somewhat skeptically as a student, moved in. That was in the autumn of 1919. Steinbeck is reticent about the details of his college career but the records at Stanford show that he withdrew in the spring of 1920, entered again in the fall and withdrew almost at once, was in residence throughout the academic year, 1922-23, and again in 1924-25. In between times he was working here and there, down on Salinas Valley ranches, in the sugar refinery again, digesting what he had got out of his courses in English and history as taught in Palo Alto, reading widely in such fields as happened to attract him, learning to roll the brown-paper cigarettes he still prefers to the machine-made article, and making up his mind about writing fiction. He did not take a degree. The next step in writing was to write.

In the middle 1920's, as before and since, New York was the place for all ambitious young writers who didn't want to go the whole hog and wind up at the Dôme. Anyway, Paris was more for the Lost Generation, and Steinbeck had just missed the war. So he chose his freight boat and departed for New York by way of the Panama Canal. On the way he learned to his astonishment that plain, ordinary, unloaded dice could be controlled if one knew how. The discovery came to him through the medium of a large and very black sailor and was slightly expensive, but at least it was something to know. He stayed over at Panama, too, picking up another boat later, in order to absorb color there for a book he had in mind, the romanticized life of the pirate, Henry Morgan, which appeared as his first book, *Cup of Gold*. But that was afterward. The net result of the dice lessons and the research was that he arrived in New York broke. The thing was to get work.

He got very little. For a while he held down a reporter's job, but that didn't last long. A metropolitan newspaper will hire young men who intend to be great writers some day, but only if the said young men are successful in feigning a consuming passion for the dirty details of a reporter's job. Steinbeck couldn't. A good deal of it seemed like out-and-out nonsense to him, and he wasn't used to being horsed around by a city editor he could break in two without half trying. So he found himself out in the street in short order. Still, he had to eat, and when a friend offered to get him a job on the new Madison Square Garden building, he took it and carried bricks as long as there were bricks to carry. Then that job folded up and Steinbeck joined the ranks of bright young fellows who poke around for ideas and try to free-lance them as pieces for the paper.

That is one of the best ways to starve in all New York; eventually he saw the point, and headed back for California.

His *Cup of Gold* was written some six or seven thousand feet up in the High Sierra during a winter job as watchman in a house on the rim of Tahoe's Emerald Bay. Once a week Steinbeck snowshoed down to the frozen brink to meet the mail boat and get supplies. The rest of the time he chopped wood to keep himself warm, concluded that not even the most conscientious watchman could have done anything about the giant sugar-pine that crashed through the roof of the big house one night when he was snug in one of the guest-cabins, and went on writing. *Cup of Gold* was his first published novel, but it was his fourth; of the others, two were never shown to any publisher, one was very thoroughly turned down, and all three are now destroyed. He wrote short stories, too, but no one wanted them. Steinbeck went on chopping wood, burning up his stories, writing others until summer came and the owners of the Tahoe house fired him for letting the pine tree fall through their roof. He got a job next day in a trout hatchery only a few miles away. He liked that work, though when you ask him why he only says vaguely, "Oh, all the little fishes!" .

Then McBride took *Cup of Gold*. That was the year the boom collapsed, but anyway Steinbeck had a new status. The book wasn't making any money at all, but at least he was a published author. He married Carol Henning of San José, California, whose parents had come from the old mining country (her grandfather built the Leland Stanford house, up in the Sierra foothills at Michigan Bluff) and went to live in a tiny house his parents gave the couple in Pacific Grove, a stone's throw from arty Carmel.

The next two years saw publication of *Pastures of Heaven* and *To a God Unknown*, both highly praised by the critics and both completely neglected by the book-buying public. Reviewers used fine strong words like "virile" and "magnifi-

cent," and referred to the author's "simple, in-
delible power," which was very good of them.
But the Steinbecks could not live on their royalties because there were no royalties to live on.
Out in Chicago Ben Abramson, the bookseller,
went into a conniption about Steinbeck and
bought up all the copies he could find of all his
books, including the stock that the publishers had
sadly remaindered. But there they stayed, on
Abramson's shelves. Nobody else, apparently, felt
at all sanguine about Steinbeck. All that most
people could see was a new kind of novelist who
never wrote two books that were anything like
each other. How can you place a fellow like
that?

However, it was Pacific Grove, on the shore
of Monterey Bay, that gave Steinbeck his key to
the public's heart at last, even to its pocketbook.
For when he wanted relaxation, in between pe-
riods of writing and morose reflection on where
the next meal was coming from, Steinbeck developed the habit of wandering up to the little settle-

ment of *paisanos* on a small hilltop overlooking the bay. Some of them were fishermen, but most were just loafers, enjoying life however they could, always able to postpone thinking about tomorrow as long as there was a jug of rough California wine to be had and a chance to sing, tell stories, or just talk. Somehow they always managed to find the wine, even in those dry days. And Steinbeck had plenty of time to talk and tell stories of his own and drink with them. Out of those *paisanos* came *Tortilla Flat*, and for the first time in their joint lives the Steinbecks had a little spare cash. In fact, they had more than a little, for in the first flush of public enthusiasm for the book, the motion-picture people bought *Tortilla Flat*. There was some talk of Steinbeck's going down to Hollywood to work on the picture, but the merest whisper of such a thing was enough to frighten him. He loaded his wife and some clothes into a second-hand Chevrolet and hit for the Mexican border. The new Pan-American highway was open, and Mexico City was a far cry from the film city. Let Hollywood try to find him.

Before he went to Mexico, he had finished *In Dubious Battle*, which many people have called the best strike novel ever written. He didn't return until that book was ready to come out. By that time, he figured, Hollywood would probably have forgotten all about asking him to come down to work on *Tortilla Flat*. He was right, too. Not only had the film executives dismissed that idea, but they had apparently dismissed the idea of making the picture at all. In fact, nothing has been done with it yet. There is a rumor that one well-known actor was offered the part of Danny but turned it down as being beneath his dignity. Maybe it is just a rumor.

In Dubious Battle had a curious reception. Again readers noted that Steinbeck had written a book that was totally unlike any other he had done. Most of them had read none of Steinbeck excepting *Tortilla Flat*, but at least this was nothing like that.

INTRODUCTION

The leftist reviewers were disappointed because there wasn't enough propaganda in Steinbeck's account of the strike. Reactionary readers were also annoyed; Steinbeck told too much about the technique of breaking strikes. Perhaps he was some kind of Red. In California the least suspicion of such a thing is enough; the public in Steinbeck's own part of the country dropped *In Dubious Battle* like a hot potato. That is, most of them did. To its credit, the Commonwealth Club of California saw the quality in the book and awarded it the Club's gold medal given annually for the best novel by a California writer during the previous year. Steinbeck was properly grateful, though he upset the Club members by declining to come and get his medal at the official medal-giving dinner. Wild horses could not have dragged him to a platform anywhere, let alone set him upright and persuade him to go through the gestures of polite acceptance. He regards speeches with horror, his own or others'. Once he was unwillingly carried by his publisher to a literary dinner. He managed to sit through the first two or three addresses, but that was all. Friends found him afterward in the hotel bar, staring fixedly into a double brandy-and-soda, still embarrassed and ashamed that men and women who could write so well could stand up in front of an audience and talk such stuff.

The point is that John Steinbeck is a simple, natural individual, not given to pose of any kind, impatient—his only impatience—of pretense anywhere. There is no mystery at all about him, which is why he has been made to seem mysterious by those who cannot understand his simplicity. He does not like publicity, does not feel that it helps him to write, helps his books, does him or anyone else any good whatever. He doesn't go to dinners for the best of reasons; he doesn't like them. He turns down cameramen because he hates being photographed. For years, Sonia Noskowiak, out on the Coast, and Peter Stackpole of *Life* were the only photographers who had taken his picture. He and his wife live very simply; not in Pacific Grove any more but farther back in the hills, away from the water entirely, in Los Gatos where they built a small house with the *Tortilla Flat* movie money and furnished it with loot from their Mexican trip.

Steinbeck has one superstition common to many writers. He will not discuss a book while he is working on it. After it is finished he is even less inclined to talk about it because it is something over and done with, and he is thinking about the next one. Perhaps that is one reason why *Of Mice and Men* was so little understood when it first appeared. The critics liked it, to be sure, but not more than one or two in the whole length and breadth of the country saw the point, though they attributed to its author all sorts of motives and purposes that had never entered his head. Steinbeck wanted to see how like a play he could write a short novel. No more and no less. And the play made from the book is proof enough that his experiment was highly successful. You can give Hollywood good marks for shrewdness, however. This time they came after Steinbeck hard. And though he considers Hollywood second only to New York as a bad place for a writer to go, he almost weakened and went. Six weeks at a thousand dollars a week makes six thousand dollars, and Steinbeck knew exactly where he could put his finger on three thousand agricultural workers down in the Valley who didn't have two dollars apiece to pay their union fees. If Pascal Covici hadn't flown out to the Coast to talk him out of it, he'd have gone, too, and for just that reason. You see, he really knows about these workers. The only time he has ever deserted fiction was once when the Scripps-Howard San Francisco *News* got him to write a series of articles about the transient labor camps in California. He has not been quite the same man since he saw how those people had to live and learned something about their problems.

But in the end he didn't go to Hollywood. Instead, he and his wife went to Scandinavia—on a freight-boat because he has the habit of freight-boats—not to write about that part of the world but because they both liked what they'd heard of it. In fact, Steinbeck felt about Norway and Sweden and Denmark and those places very much as he felt when he went to work in the trout hatchery. They sounded interesting. All those little fishes.

OF MICE AND MEN

I

A FEW MILES south of Soledad, the Salinas River drops in close to the hillside bank and runs deep and green. The water is warm too, for it has slipped twinkling over the yellow sands in the sunlight before reaching the narrow pool. On one side of the river the golden foothill slopes curve up to the strong and rocky Gabilan mountains, but on the valley side the water is lined with trees—willows fresh and green with every spring, carrying in their lower leaf junctures the debris of the winter's flooding; and sycamores with mottled, white, recumbent limbs and branches that arch over the pool. On the sandy bank under the trees the leaves lie deep and so crisp that a lizard makes a great skittering if he runs among them. Rabbits come out of the brush to sit on the sand in the evening, and the damp flats are covered with the night tracks of 'coons, and with the spread pads of dogs from the ranches, and with the split-wedge tracks of deer that come to drink in the dark.

There is a path through the willows and among the sycamores, a path beaten hard by boys coming down from the ranches to swim in the deep pool, and beaten hard by tramps who come wearily down from the highway in the evening to jungle-up near water. In front of the low horizontal limb of a giant sycamore there is an ash pile made by many fires; the limb is worn smooth by men who have sat on it.

Evening of a hot day started the little wind to moving among the leaves. The shade climbed up the hills toward the top. On the sand banks the rabbits sat as quietly as little gray, sculptured stones. And then from the direction of the state highway came the sound of footsteps on crisp sycamore leaves. The rabbits hurried noiselessly for cover. A stilted heron labored up into the air and pounded down river. For a moment the place was lifeless, and then two men emerged from the path and came into the opening by the green pool.

They had walked in single file down the path, and even in the open one stayed behind the other. Both were dressed in denim trousers and in denim coats with brass buttons. Both wore black, shapeless hats and both carried tight blanket rolls slung over their shoulders. The first man was small and quick, dark of face, with restless eyes and sharp, strong features. Every part of him was defined: small, strong hands, slender arms, a thin and bony nose. Behind him walked his opposite, a huge man, shapeless of face, with large, pale eyes, with wide, sloping shoulders; and he walked heavily, dragging his feet a little, the way a bear drags his paws. His arms did not swing at his sides, but hung loosely.

The first man stopped short in the clearing,

9

and the follower nearly ran over him. He took off his hat and wiped the sweat-band with his forefinger and snapped the moisture off. His huge companion dropped his blankets and flung himself down and drank from the surface of the green pool; drank with long gulps, snorting into the water like a horse. The small man stepped nervously beside him.

"Lennie!" he said sharply. "Lennie, for God' sakes don't drink so much." Lennie continued to snort into the pool. The small man leaned over and shook him by the shoulder. "Lennie. You gonna be sick like you was last night."

Lennie dipped his whole head under, hat and all, and then he sat up on the bank and his hat dripped down on his blue coat and ran down his back. "Tha's good," he said. "You drink some, George. You take a good big drink." He smiled happily.

George unslung his bindle and dropped it gently on the bank. "I ain't sure it's good water," he said. "Looks kinda scummy."

Lennie dabbled his big paw in the water and wiggled his fingers so the water arose in little splashes; rings widened across the pool to the other side and came back again. Lennie watched them go. "Look, George. Look what I done."

George knelt beside the pool and drank from his hand with quick scoops. "Tastes all right," he admitted. "Don't really seem to be running, though. You never oughta drink water when it ain't running, Lennie," he said hopelessly. "You'd drink out of a gutter if you was thirsty." He threw a scoop of water into his face and rubbed it about with his hand, under his chin and around the back of his neck. Then he replaced his hat, pushed himself back from the river, drew up his knees and embraced them. Lennie, who had been watching, imitated George exactly. He pushed himself back, drew up his knees, embraced them, looked over to George to see whether he had it just right. He pulled his hat down a little more over his eyes, the way George's hat was.

11

George stared morosely at the water. The rims of his eyes were red with sun glare. He said angrily, "We could just as well of rode clear to the ranch if that bastard bus driver knew what he was talkin' about. 'Jes' a little stretch down the highway,' he says. 'Jes' a little stretch.' God damn near four miles, that's what it was! Didn't wanta stop at the ranch gate, that's what. Too God damn lazy to pull up. Wonder he isn't too damn good to stop in Soledad at all. Kicks us out and says, 'Jes' a little stretch down the road.' I bet it was *more* than four miles. Damn hot day."

Lennie looked timidly over to him. "George?"

"Yeah, what ya want?"

"Where we goin', George?"

The little man jerked down the brim of his hat and scowled over at Lennie. "So you forgot that awready, did you? I gotta tell you again, do I? Jesus Christ, you're a crazy bastard!"

"I forgot," Lennie said softly. "I tried not to forget. Honest to God I did, George."

12

"O.K.—O.K. I'll tell ya again. I ain't got nothing to do. Might jus' as well spen' all my time tellin' you things and then you forget 'em, and I tell you again."

"Tried and tried," said Lennie, "but it didn't do no good. I remember about the rabbits, George."

"The hell with the rabbits. That's all you ever can remember is them rabbits. O.K! Now you listen and this time you got to remember so we don't get in no trouble. You remember settin' in that gutter on Howard street and watchin' that blackboard?"

Lennie's face broke into a delighted smile. "Why sure, George. I remember that . . . . but . . . . what'd we do then? I remember some girls come by and you says . . . . you say . . . ."

"The hell with what I says. You remember about us goin' into Murray and Ready's, and they give us work cards and bus tickets?"

"Oh, sure, George. I remember that now." His hands went quickly into his side coat pockets. He said gently, "George . . . . I ain't got mine. I musta lost it." He looked down at the ground in despair.

"You never had none, you crazy bastard. I got both of 'em here. Think I'd let you carry your own work card?"

Lennie grinned with relief. "I . . . . I thought I put it in my side pocket." His hand went into the pocket again.

George looked sharply at him. "What'd you take outa that pocket?"

"Ain't a thing in my pocket," Lennie said cleverly.

"I know there ain't. You got it in your hand. What you got in your hand—hidin' it?"

"I ain't got nothin', George. Honest."

"Come on, give it here."

Lennie held his closed hand away from George's direction. "It's on'y a mouse, George."

"A mouse? A live mouse?"

"Uh-uh. Jus' a dead mouse, George. I didn' kill it. Honest! I found it. I found it dead."

"Give it here!" said George.

"Aw, leave me have it, George."

"Give it here!"

Lennie's closed hand slowly obeyed. George took the mouse and threw it across the pool to the other side, among the brush. "What you want of a dead mouse, anyways?"

"I could pet it with my thumb while we walked along," said Lennie.

"Well, you ain't petting no mice while you walk with me. You remember where we're goin' now?"

Lennie looked startled and then in embarrassment hid his face against his knees. "I forgot again."

"Jesus Christ," George said resignedly. "Well —look, we're gonna work on a ranch like the one we come from up north."

"Up north?"

"In Weed."

"Oh, sure. I remember. In Weed."

"That ranch we're goin' to is right **down**

there about a quarter mile. We're gonna go in an' see the boss. Now, look—I'll give him the work tickets, but you ain't gonna say a word. You jus' stand there and don't say nothing. If he finds out what a crazy bastard you are, we won't get no job, but if he sees ya work before he hears ya talk, we're set. Ya got that?"

"Sure, George. Sure I got it."

"O.K. Now when we go in to see the boss, what you gonna do?"

"I . . . . I," Lennie thought. His face grew tight with thought. "I . . . . ain't gonna say nothin'. Jus' gonna stan' there."

"Good boy. That's swell. You say that over two, three times so you sure won't forget it."

Lennie droned to himself softly, "I ain't gonna say nothin' . . . . I ain't gonna say nothin' . . . . I ain't gonna say nothin'."

"O.K.," said George. "An' you ain't gonna do no bad things like you done in Weed, neither."

Lennie looked puzzled. "Like I done in Weed?"

"Oh, so ya forgot that too, did ya? Well, I ain't gonna remind ya, fear ya do it again."

A light of understanding broke on Lennie's face. "They run us outa Weed," he exploded triumphantly.

"Run us out, hell," said George disgustedly. "We run. They was lookin' for us, but they didn't catch us."

Lennie giggled happily. "I didn't forget that, you bet."

George lay back on the sand and crossed his hands under his head, and Lennie imitated him, raising his head to see whether he were doing it right. "God, you're a lot of trouble," said George. "I could get along so easy and so nice if I didn't have you on my tail. I could live so easy and maybe have a girl."

For a moment Lennie lay quiet, and then he said hopefully, "We gonna work on a ranch, George."

"Awright. You got that. But we're gonna sleep here because I got a reason."

The day was going fast now. Only the tops of the Gabilan mountains flamed with the light of the sun that had gone from the valley. A water snake slipped along on the pool, its head held up like a little periscope. The reeds jerked slightly in the current. Far off toward the highway a man shouted something, and another man shouted back. The sycamore limbs rustled under a little wind that died immediately.

"George—why ain't we goin' on to the ranch and get some supper? They got supper at the ranch."

George rolled on his side. "No reason at all for you. I like it here. Tomorra we're gonna go to work. I seen thrashin' machines on the way down. That means we'll be bucking grain bags, bustin' a gut. Tonight I'm gonna lay right here and look up. I like it."

Lennie got up on his knees and looked down at George. "Ain't we gonna have no supper?"

"Sure we are, if you gather up some dead willow sticks. I got three cans of beans in my

18

bindle. You get a fire ready. I'll give you a match when you get the sticks together. Then we'll heat the beans and have supper."

Lennie said, "I like beans with ketchup."

"Well, we ain't got no ketchup. You go get wood. An' don't you fool around. It'll be dark before long."

Lennie lumbered to his feet and disappeared in the brush. George lay where he was and whistled softly to himself. There were sounds of splashings down the river in the direction Lennie had taken. George stopped whistling and listened. "Poor bastard," he said softly, and then went on whistling again.

In a moment Lennie came crashing back through the brush. He carried one small willow stick in his hand. George sat up. "Awright," he said brusquely. "Gi'me that mouse!"

But Lennie made an elaborate pantomime of innocence. "What mouse, George? I ain't got no mouse."

George held out his hand. "Come on. Give it to me. You ain't puttin' nothing over."

Lennie hesitated, backed away, looked wildly at the brush line as though he contemplated running for his freedom. George said coldly, "You gonna give me that mouse or do I have to sock you?"

"Give you what, George?"

"You know God damn well what. I want that mouse."

Lennie reluctantly reached into his pocket. His voice broke a little. "I don't know why I can't keep it. It ain't nobody's mouse. I didn't steal it. I found it lyin' right beside the road."

George's hand remained outstretched imperiously. Slowly, like a terrier who doesn't want to bring a ball to its master, Lennie approached, drew back, approached again. George snapped his fingers sharply, and at the sound Lennie laid the mouse in his hand.

"I wasn't doin' nothing bad with it, George. Jus' strokin' it."

George stood up and threw the mouse as far as he could into the darkening brush, and then he stepped to the pool and washed his hands. "You crazy fool. Don't you think I could see your feet was wet where you went acrost the river to get it?" He heard Lennie's whimpering cry and wheeled about. "Blubberin' like a baby! Jesus Christ! A big guy like you." Lennie's lip quivered and tears started in his eyes. "Aw, Lennie!" George put his hand on Lennie's shoulder. "I ain't takin' it away jus' for meanness. That mouse ain't fresh, Lennie; and besides, you've broke it pettin' it. You get another mouse that's fresh and I'll let you keep it a little while."

Lennie sat down on the ground and hung his head dejectedly. "I don't know where there is no other mouse. I remember a lady used to give 'em to me—ever' one she got. But that lady ain't here."

George scoffed. "Lady, huh? Don't even remember who that lady was. That was your own Aunt Clara. An' she stopped givin' 'em to ya. You always killed 'em."

Lennie looked sadly up at him. "They was so

little," he said, apologetically. "I'd pet 'em, and pretty soon they bit my fingers and I pinched their heads a little and then they was dead— because they was so little."

"I wish't we'd get the rabbits pretty soon, George. They ain't so little."

"The hell with the rabbits. An' you ain't to be trusted with no live mice. Your Aunt Clara give you a rubber mouse and you wouldn't have nothing to do with it."

"It wasn't no good to pet," said Lennie.

The flame of the sunset lifted from the mountaintops and dusk came into the valley, and a half darkness came in among the willows and the sycamores. A big carp rose to the surface of the pool, gulped air and then sank mysteriously into the dark water again, leaving widening rings on the water. Overhead the leaves whisked again and little puffs of willow cotton blew down and landed on the pool's surface.

"You gonna get that wood?" George demanded. "There's plenty right up against the back of that sycamore. Floodwater wood. Now you get it."

Lennie went behind the tree and brought out a litter of dried leaves and twigs. He threw them in a heap on the old ash pile and went back for more and more. It was almost night now. A dove's wings whistled over the water. George walked to the fire pile and lighted the dry leaves. The flame cracked up among the twigs and fell to work. George undid his bindle and brought out three cans of beans. He stood them about the fire, close in against the blaze, but not quite touching the flame.

"There's enough beans for four men," George said.

Lennie watched him from over the fire. He said patiently, "I like 'em with ketchup."

"Well, we ain't got any," George exploded. "Whatever we ain't got, that's what you want. God a'mighty, if I was alone I could live so easy. I could go get a job an' work, an' no trouble. No mess at all, and when the end of the month come I could take my fifty bucks and go into town and get whatever I want. Why, I could stay in a cat house all night. I could eat any place I want, hotel or any place, and order any damn thing I could think of. An' I could do all that every damn month. Get a gallon of whisky, or set in a pool room and play cards or shoot pool." Lennie knelt and looked over the fire at the angry George. And Lennie's face was drawn with terror. "An' whatta I got," George went on furiously. "I got you! You can't keep a job and you lose me ever' job I get. Jus' keep me shovin' all over the country all the time. An' that ain't the worst. You get in trouble. You do bad things and I got to get you out." His voice rose nearly to a shout. "You crazy son-of-a-bitch. You keep me in hot water all the time." He took on the elaborate manner of little girls when they are mimicking one another. "Jus' wanted to feel that girl's dress—jus' wanted to pet it like it was a mouse—— Well, how the hell did she know you jus' wanted to feel her dress?

24

She jerks back and you hold on like it was a mouse. She yells and we got to hide in a irrigation ditch all day with guys lookin' for us, and we got to sneak out in the dark and get outta the country. All the time somethin' like that—all the time. I wisht I could put you in a cage with about a million mice an' let you have fun." His anger left him suddenly. He looked across the fire at Lennie's anguished face, and then he looked ashamedly at the flames.

It was quite dark now, but the fire lighted the trunks of the trees and the curving branches overhead. Lennie crawled slowly and cautiously around the fire until he was close to George. He sat back on his heels. George turned the bean cans so that another side faced the fire. He pretended to be unaware of Lennie so close beside him.

"George," very softly. No answer. "George!"

"Whatta you want?"

"I was only foolin', George. I don't want no ketchup. I wouldn't eat no ketchup if it was right here beside me."

"If it was here, you could have some."

"But I wouldn't eat none, George. I'd leave it all for you. You could cover your beans with it and I wouldn't touch none of it."

George still stared morosely at the fire. "When I think of the swell time I could have without you, I go nuts. I never get no peace."

Lennie still knelt. He looked off into the darkness across the river. "George, you want I should go away and leave you alone?"

"Where the hell could you go?"

"Well, I could. I could go off in the hills there. Some place I'd find a cave."

"Yeah? How'd you eat. You ain't got sense enough to find nothing to eat."

"I'd find things, George. I don't need no nice food with ketchup. I'd lay out in the sun and nobody'd hurt me. An' if I foun' a mouse, I could keep it. Nobody'd take it away from me."

George looked quickly and searchingly at him. "I been mean, ain't I?"

"If you don' want me I can go off in the hills

an' find a cave. I can go away any time."

"No—look! I was jus' foolin', Lennie. 'Cause I want you to stay with me. Trouble with mice is you always kill 'em. " He paused. "Tell you what I'll do, Lennie. First chance I get I'll give you a pup. Maybe you wouldn't kill *it*. That'd be better than mice. And you could pet it harder."

Lennie avoided the bait. He had sensed his advantage. "If you don't want me, you only jus' got to say so, and I'll go off in those hills right there—right up in those hills and live by myself. An' I won't get no mice stole from me."

George said, "I want you to stay with me, Lennie. Jesus Christ, somebody'd shoot you for a coyote if you was by yourself. No, you stay with me. Your Aunt Clara wouldn't like you running off by yourself, even if she is dead."

Lennie spoke craftily, "Tell me—like you done before."

"Tell you what?"

"About the rabbits."

27

George snapped, "You ain't gonna put nothing over on me."

Lennie pleaded, "Come on, George. Tell me. Please, George. Like you done before."

"You get a kick outta that, don't you? Awright, I'll tell you, and then we'll eat our supper. . . ."

George's voice became deeper. He repeated his words rhythmically as though he had said them many times before. "Guys like us, that work on ranches, are the loneliest guys in the world. They got no family. They don't belong no place. They come to a ranch an' work up a stake and then they go inta town and blow their stake, and the first thing you know they're poundin' their tail on some other ranch. They ain't got nothing to look ahead to."

Lennie was delighted. 'That's it—that's it. Now tell how it is with us."

George went on. "With us it ain't like that. We got a future. We got somebody to talk to that gives a damn about us. We don't have to sit in no bar room blowin' in our jack jus' because we got no place else to go. If them other guys gets in jail they can rot for all anybody gives a damn. But not us."

Lennie broke in. *"But not us! An' why? Because . . . . because I got you to look after me, and you got me to look after you, and that's why."* He laughed delightedly. "Go on now, George!"

"You got it by heart. You can do it yourself."

"No, you. I forget some a' the things. Tell about how it's gonna be."

"O.K. Someday—we're gonna get the jack together and we're gonna have a little house and a couple of acres an' a cow and some pigs and——"

"An' live off the fatta the lan'," Lennie shouted. "An' have *rabbits*. Go on, George! Tell about what we're gonna have in the garden and about the rabbits in the cages and about the rain in the winter and the stove, and how thick the

29

cream is on the milk like you can hardly cut it. Tell about that, George."

"Why'n't you do it yourself? You know all of it."

"No . . . . you tell it. It ain't the same if I tell it. Go on . . . . George. How I get to tend the rabbits."

"Well," said George, "we'll have a big vegetable patch and a rabbit hutch and chickens. And when it rains in the winter, we'll just say the hell with goin' to work, and we'll build up a fire in the stove and set around it an' listen to the rain comin' down on the roof—Nuts!" He took out his pocket knife. "I ain't got time for no more." He drove his knife through the top of one of the bean cans, sawed out the top and passed the can to Lennie. Then he opened a second can. From his side pocket he brought out two spoons and passed one of them to Lennie.

They sat by the fire and filled their mouths with beans and chewed mightily. A few beans slipped out of the side of Lennie's mouth.

George gestured with his spoon. "What you gonna say tomorrow when the boss asks you questions?"

Lennie stopped chewing and swallowed. His face was concentrated. "I . . . . I ain't gonna . . . . say a word."

"Good boy! That's fine, Lennie! Maybe you're gettin' better. When we get the coupla acres I can let you tend the rabbits all right. 'Specially if you remember as good as that."

Lennie choked with pride. "I can remember," he said.

George motioned with his spoon again. "Look, Lennie. I want you to look around here. You can remember this place, can't you? The ranch is about a quarter mile up that way. Just follow the river?"

"Sure," said Lennie. "I can remember this. Di'n't I remember about not gonna say a word?"

" 'Course you did. Well, look. Lennie—if you jus' happen to get in trouble like you always

done before, I want you to come right here an'
hide in the brush."

"Hide in the brush," said Lennie slowly.

"Hide in the brush till I come for you. Can
you remember that?"

"Sure I can, George. Hide in the brush till
you come."

"But you ain't gonna get in no trouble, because if you do, I won't let you tend the rabbits." He threw his empty bean can off into
the brush.

"I won't get in no trouble, George. I ain't
gonna say a word."

"O.K. Bring your bindle over here by the
fire. It's gonna be nice sleepin' here. Lookin' up,
and the leaves. Don't build up no more fire.
We'll let her die down."

They made their beds on the sand, and as the
blaze dropped from the fire the sphere of light
grew smaller; the curling branches disappeared
and only a faint glimmer showed where the tree
trunks were. From the darkness Lennie called,
"George—you asleep?"

32

"No. Whatta you want?"

"Let's have different color rabbits, George."

"Sure we will," George said sleepily. "Red and blue and green rabbits, Lennie. Millions of 'em."

"Furry ones, George, like I seen in the fair in Sacramento."

"Sure, furry ones."

" 'Cause I can jus' as well go away, George, an' live in a cave."

"You can jus' as well go to hell," said George. "Shut up now."

The red light dimmed on the coals. Up the hill from the river a coyote yammered, and a dog answered from the other side of the stream. The sycamore leaves whispered in a little night breeze.

2

THE bunk house was a long, rectangular building. Inside, the walls were whitewashed and the
floor unpainted. In three walls there were small,
square windows, and in the fourth, a solid door
with a wooden latch. Against the walls were
eight bunks, five of them made up with blankets
and the other three showing their burlap ticking.
Over each bunk there was nailed an apple box
with the opening forward so that it made two
shelves for the personal belongings of the oc-
cupant of the bunk. And these shelves were
loaded with little articles, soap and talcum powder, razors and those Western magazines ranch
men love to read and scoff at and secretly be-
lieve. And there were medicines on the shelves,
and little vials, combs; and from nails on the

box sides, a few neckties. Near one wall there was a black cast-iron stove, its stovepipe going straight up through the ceiling. In the middle of the room stood a big square table littered with playing cards, and around it were grouped boxes for the players to sit on.

At about ten o'clock in the morning the sun threw a bright dust-laden bar through one of the side windows, and in and out of the beam flies shot like rushing stars.

The wooden latch raised. The door opened and a tall, stoop-shouldered old man came in. He was dressed in blue jeans and he carried a big push-broom in his left hand. Behind him came George, and behind George, Lennie.

"The boss was expectin' you last night," the old man said. "He was sore as hell when you wasn't here to go out this morning." He pointed with his right arm, and out of the sleeve came a round stick-like wrist, but no hand. "You can have them two beds there," he said, indicating two bunks near the stove.

35

George stepped over and threw his blankets down on the burlap sack of straw that was a mattress. He looked into his box shelf and then picked a small yellow can from it. "Say. What the hell's this?"

"I don't know," said the old man.

"Says 'positively kills lice, roaches and other scourges.' What the hell kind of bed you giving us, anyways. We don't want no pants rabbits."

The old swamper shifted his broom and held it between his elbow and his side while he held out his hand for the can. He studied the label carefully. "Tell you what—" he said finally, "last guy that had this bed was a blacksmith— hell of a nice fella and as clean a guy as you want to meet. Used to wash his hands even *after* he ate."

"Then how come he got graybacks?" George was working up a slow anger. Lennie put his bindle on the neighboring bunk and sat down. He watched George with open mouth.

"Tell you what," said the old swamper. "This

here blacksmith—name of Whitey—was the kind of guy that would put that stuff around even if there wasn't no bugs—just to make sure, see? Tell you what he used to do— At meals he'd peel his boil' potatoes, an' he'd take out ever' little spot, no matter what kind, before he'd eat it. And if there was a red splotch on an egg, he'd scrape it off. Finally quit about the food. That's the kinda guy he was—clean. Used ta dress up Sundays even when he wasn't going no place, put on a necktie even, and then set in the bunkhouse."

"I ain't so sure," said George skeptically. "What did you say he quit for?"

The old man put the yellow can in his pocket, and he rubbed his bristly white whiskers with his knuckles. "Why . . . . he . . . . just quit, the way a guy will. Says it was the food. Just wanted to move. Didn't give no other reason but the food. Just says 'gimme my time' one night, the way any guy would."

George lifted his tick and looked underneath

it. He leaned over and inspected the sacking closely. Immediately Lennie got up and did the same with his bed. Finally George seemed satisfied. He unrolled his bindle and put things on the shelf, his razor and bar of soap, his comb and bottle of pills, his liniment and leather wristband. Then he made his bed up neatly with blankets. The old man said, "I guess the boss'll be out here in a minute. He was sure burned when you wasn't here this morning. Come right in when we was eatin' breakfast and says, 'Where the hell's them new men?' An' he give the stable buck hell, too."

George patted a wrinkle out of his bed, and sat down. "Give the stable buck hell?" he asked.

"Sure. Ya see the stable buck's a nigger."

"Nigger, huh?"

"Yeah. Nice fella too. Got a crooked back where a horse kicked him. The boss gives him hell when he's mad. But the stable buck don't give a damn about that. He reads a lot. Got books in his room."

"What kind of a guy is the boss?" George asked.

"Well, he's a pretty nice fella. Gets pretty mad sometimes, but he's pretty nice. Tell ya what—know what he done Christmas? Brang a gallon of whisky right in here and says, 'Drink hearty boys. Christmas comes but once a year.'"

"The hell he did! Whole gallon?"

"Yes sir. Jesus, we had fun. They let the nigger come in that night. Little skinner name of Smitty took after the nigger. Done pretty good, too. The guys wouldn't let him use his feet, so the nigger got him. If he coulda used his feet, Smitty says he woulda killed the nigger. The guys said on account of the nigger's got a crooked back, Smitty can't use his feet." He paused in relish of the memory. "After that the guys went into Soledad and raised hell. I didn't go in there. I ain't got the poop no more."

Lennie was just finishing making his bed. The wooden latch raised again and the door opened. A little stocky man stood in the open doorway.

He wore blue jean trousers, a flannel shirt, a black, unbuttoned vest and a black coat. His thumbs were stuck in his belt, on each side of a square steel buckle. On his head was a soiled brown Stetson hat, and he wore high-heeled boots and spurs to prove he was not a laboring man.

The old swamper looked quickly at him, and then shuffled to the door rubbing his whiskers with his knuckles as he went. "Them guys just come," he said, and shuffled past the boss and out the door.

The boss stepped into the room with the short, quick steps of a fat-legged man. "I wrote Murray and Ready I wanted two men this morning. You got your work slips?" George reached into his pocket and produced the slips and handed them to the boss. "It wasn't Murray and Ready's fault. Says right here on the slip that you was to be here for work this morning."

George looked down at his feet. "Bus driver

give us a bum steer," he said. "We hadda walk ten miles. Says we was here when we wasn't. We couldn't get no rides in the morning."

The boss squinted his eyes. "Well, I had to send out the grain teams short two buckers. Won't do any good to go out now till after dinner." He pulled his time book out of his pocket and opened it where a pencil was stuck between the leaves. George scowled meaningfully at Lennie, and Lennie nodded to show that he understood. The boss licked his pencil. "What's your name?"

"George Milton."

"And what's yours?"

George said, "His name's Lennie Small."

The names were entered in the book. "Le's see, this is the twentieth, noon the twentieth." He closed the book. "Where you boys been working?"

"Up around Weed," said George.

"You, too?" to Lennie.

"Yeah, him too," said George.

The boss pointed a playful finger at **Lennie.**
"He ain't much of a talker, is he?"

"No, he ain't, but he's sure a hell of a good
worker. Strong as a bull."

Lennie smiled to himself. "Strong as a bull,"
he repeated.

George scowled at him, and Lennie dropped
his head in shame at having forgotten.

The boss said suddenly, "Listen, Small!" Lennie raised his head. "What can you do?"

In a panic, Lennie looked at George for help.
"He can do anything you tell him," said George.
"He's a good skinner. He can rassel grain bags,
drive a cultivator. He can do anything. Just give
him a try."

The boss turned on George. "Then why don't
you let him answer? What you trying to put
over?"

George broke in loudly, "Oh! I ain't saying
he's bright. He ain't. But I say he's a God damn
good worker. He can put up a four hundred
pound bale."

The boss deliberately put the little book in his pocket. He hooked his thumbs in his belt and squinted one eye nearly closed. "Say—what you sellin'?"

"Huh?"

"I said what stake you got in this guy? You takin' his pay away from him?"

"No, 'course I ain't. Why ya think I'm sellin' him out?"

"Well, I never seen one guy take so much trouble for another guy. I just like to know what your interest is."

George said, "He's my . . . . cousin. I told his old lady I'd take care of him. He got kicked in the head by a horse when he was a kid. He's awright. Just ain't bright. But he can do anything you tell him."

The boss turned half away. "Well, God knows he don't need any brains to buck barley bags. But don't you try to put nothing over, Milton. I got my eye on you. Why'd you quit in Weed?"

43

"Job was done," said George promptly.

"What kinda job?"

"We . . . . we was diggin' a cesspool."

"All right. But don't try to put nothing over, 'cause you can't get away with nothing. I seen wise guys before. Go on out with the grain teams after dinner. They're pickin' up barley at the threshing machine. Go out with Slim's team."

"Slim?"

"Yeah. Big tall skinner. You'll see him at dinner." He turned abruptly and went to the door, but before he went out he turned and looked for a long moment at the two men.

When the sound of his footsteps had died away, George turned on Lennie. "So you wasn't gonna say a word. You was gonna leave your big flapper shut and leave me do the talkin'. Damn near lost us the job."

Lennie stared hopelessly at his hands. "I forgot, George."

"Yeah, you forgot. You always forget, an' I

got to talk you out of it." He sat down heavily on the bunk. "Now he's got his eye on us. Now we got to be careful and not make no slips. You keep your big flapper shut after this." He fell morosely silent.

"George."

"What you want now?"

"I wasn't kicked in the head with no horse, was I, George?"

"Be a damn good thing if you was," George said viciously. "Save ever'body a hell of a lot of trouble."

"You said I was your cousin, George."

"Well, that was a lie. An' I'm damn glad it was. If I was a relative of yours I'd shoot myself." He stopped suddenly, stepped to the open front door and peered out. "Say, what the hell you doin' listenin'?"

The old man came slowly into the room. He had his broom in his hand. And at his heels there walked a dragfooted sheepdog, gray of muzzle, and with pale, blind old eyes. The dog strug-

45

gled lamely to the side of the room and lay down, grunting softly to himself and licking his grizzled, moth-eaten coat. The swamper watched him until he was settled. "I wasn't listenin'. I was jus' standin' in the shade a minute scratchin' my dog. I jus' now finished swampin' out the wash house."

"You was pokin' your big ears into our business," George said. "I don't like nobody to get nosey."

The old man looked uneasily from George to Lennie, and then back. "I jus' come there," he said. "I didn't hear nothing you guys was sayin'. I ain't interested in nothing you was sayin'. A guy on a ranch don't never listen nor he don't ast no questions."

"Damn right he don't," said George, slightly mollified, "not if he wants to stay workin' long." But he was reassured by the swamper's defense. "Come on in and set down a minute," he said. "That's a hell of an old dog."

"Yeah. I had 'im ever since he was a pup. God,

he was a good sheep dog when he was younger. "
He stood his broom against the wall and he
rubbed his white bristled cheek with his
knuckles. "How'd you like the boss?" he asked.

"Pretty good. Seemed awright."

"He's a nice fella," the swamper agreed. "You
got to take him right."

At that moment a young man came into the
bunk house; a thin young man with a brown
face, with brown eyes and a head of tightly
curled hair. He wore a work glove on his left
hand, and, like the boss, he wore high-heeled
boots. "Seen my old man?" he asked.

The swamper said, "He was here jus' a minute
ago, Curley. Went over to the cook house, I
think."

"I'll try to catch him," said Curley. His eyes
passed over the new men and he stopped. He
glanced coldly at George and then at Lennie.
His arms gradually bent at the elbows and his
hands closed into fists. He stiffened and went
into a slight crouch. His glance was at once

47

calculating and pugnacious. Lennie squirmed under the look and shifted his feet nervously. Curley stepped gingerly close to him. "You the new guys the old man was waitin' for?"

"We just come in," said George.

"Let the big guy talk."

Lennie twisted with embarrassment.

George said, "S'pose he don't want to talk?"

Curley lashed his body around. "By Christ, he's gotta talk when he's spoke to. What the hell are you gettin' into it for?"

"We travel together," said George coldly.

"Oh, so it's that way."

George was tense, and motionless. "Yeah, it's that way."

Lennie was looking helplessly to George for instruction.

"An' you won't let the big guy talk, is that it?"

"He can talk if he wants to tell you anything." He nodded slightly to Lennie.

"We jus' come in," said Lennie softly.

Curley stared levelly at him. "Well, nex' time you answer when you're spoke to." He turned toward the door and walked out, and his elbows were still bent out a little.

George watched him out, and then he turned back to the swamper. "Say, what the hell's he got on his shoulder? Lennie didn't do nothing to him."

The old man looked cautiously at the door to make sure no one was listening. "That's the boss's son," he said quietly. "Curley's pretty handy. He done quite a bit in the ring. He's a lightweight, and he's handy."

"Well, let him be handy," said George. "He don't have to take after Lennie. Lennie didn't do nothing to him. What's he got against Lennie?"

The swamper considered. . . . . "Well . . . . tell you what. Curley's like a lot of little guys. He hates big guys. He's alla time picking scraps with big guys. Kind of like he's mad at 'em because he ain't a big guy. You seen little guys like that, ain't you? Always scrappy?"

"Sure," said George. "I seen plenty tough little guys. But this Curley better not make no mistakes about Lennie. Lennie ain't handy, but this Curley punk is gonna get hurt if he messes around with Lennie."

"Well, Curley's pretty handy," the swamper said skeptically. "Never did seem right to me. S'pose Curley jumps a big guy an' licks him. Ever'body says what a game guy Curley is. And s'pose he does the same thing and gets licked. Then ever'body says the big guy oughtta pick somebody his own size, and maybe they gang up on the big guy. Never did seem right to me. Seems like Curley ain't givin' nobody a chance."

George was watching the door. He said ominously, "Well, he better watch out for Lennie. Lennie ain't no fighter, but Lennie's strong and quick and Lennie don't know no rules." He walked to the square table and sat down on one of the boxes. He gathered some of the cards together and shuffled them.

The old man sat down on another box.

"Don't tell Curley I said none of this. He'd slough me. He just don't give a damn. Won't ever get canned 'cause his old man's the boss."

George cut the cards and began turning them over, looking at each one and throwing it down on a pile. He said, "This guy Curley sounds like a son-of-a-bitch to me. I don't like mean little guys."

"Seems to me like he's worse lately," said the swamper. "He got married a couple of weeks ago. Wife lives over in the boss's house. Seems like Curley is cockier'n ever since he got married."

George grunted, "Maybe he's showin' off for his wife."

The swamper warmed to his gossip. "You seen that glove on his left hand?"

"Yeah. I seen it."

"Well, that glove's fulla vaseline."

"Vaseline? What the hell for?"

"Well, I tell ya what—Curley says he's keepin' that hand soft for his wife."

George studied the cards absorbedly. "That's a dirty thing to tell around," he said.

The old man was reassured. He had drawn a derogatory statement from George. He felt safe now, and he spoke more confidently. "Wait'll you see Curley's wife."

George cut the cards again and put out a solitaire lay, slowly and deliberately. "Purty?" he asked casually.

"Yeah. Purty . . . . but——"

George studied his cards. "But what?"

"Well—she got the eye."

"Yeah? Married two weeks and got the eye? Maybe that's why Curley's pants is full of ants."

"I seen her give Slim the eye. Slim's a jerk-line skinner. Hell of a nice fella. Slim don't need to wear no high-heeled boots on a grain team. I seen her give Slim the eye. Curley never seen it. An' I seen her give Carlson the eye."

George pretended a lack of interest. "Looks like we was gonna have fun."

The swamper stood up from his box. "Know

what I think?" George did not answer. "Well, I think Curley's married . . . . a tart."

"He ain't the first," said George. "There's plenty done that."

The old man moved toward the door, and his ancient dog lifted his head and peered about, and then got painfully to his feet to follow. "I gotta be settin' out the wash basins for the guys. The teams'll be in before long. You guys gonna buck barley?"

"Yeah."

"You won't tell Curley nothing I said?"

"Hell no."

"Well, you look her over, mister. You see if she ain't a tart." He stepped out the door into the brilliant sunshine.

George laid down his cards thoughtfully, turned his piles of three. He built four clubs on his ace pile. The sun square was on the floor now, and the flies whipped through it like sparks. A sound of jingling harness and the croak of heavy-laden axles sounded from outside. From the distance came a clear call. "Stable Buck—ooh, sta-able Buck! And then, "Where the hell is that God damn nigger?"

George stared at his solitaire lay, and then he flounced the cards together and turned around to Lennie. Lennie was lying down on the bunk watching him.

"Look, Lennie! This here ain't no set up. I'm scared. You gonna have trouble with that Curley guy. I seen that kind before. He was kinda feelin' you out. He figures he's got you scared and he's gonna take a sock at you the first chance he gets."

Lennie's eyes were frightened. "I don't want no trouble," he said plaintively. "Don't let him sock me, George."

George got up and went over to Lennie's bunk and sat down on it. "I hate that kinda bastard," he said. "I seen plenty of 'em. Like the old guy says, Curley don't take no chances. He always wins." He thought for a moment. "If he tangles with you, Lennie, we're gonna get the can. Don't make no mistake about that. He's the boss's son. Look, Lennie. You try to keep away from him, will you? Don't never speak to him. If he comes in here you move clear to the other side of the room. Will you do that, Lennie?"

"I don't want no trouble," Lennie mourned. "I never done nothing to him."

"Well, that won't do you no good if Curley wants to plug himself up for a fighter. Just don't have nothing to do with him. Will you remember?"

"Sure, George. I ain't gonna say a word."

The sound of the approaching grain teams was louder, thud of big hooves on hard ground, drag of brakes and the jingle of trace chains. Men were calling back and forth from the teams. George, sitting on the bunk beside Lennie, frowned as he thought. Lennie asked timidly, "You ain't mad, George?"

"I ain't mad at you. I'm mad at this here Curley bastard. I hoped we was gonna get a little stake together—maybe a hundred dollars." His tone grew decisive. "You keep away from Curley, Lennie."

"Sure I will, George. I won't say a word."

"Don't let him pull you in—but—if the son-of-a-bitch socks you—let 'im have it."

"Let 'im have what, George?"

"Never mind, never mind. I'll tell you when. I hate that kind of a guy. Look, Lennie, if you get in any kind of trouble, you remember what I told you to do?"

Lennie raised up on his elbow. His face contorted with thought. Then his eyes moved sadly to George's face. "If I get in any trouble, you ain't gonna let me tend the rabbits."

"That's not what I meant. You remember where we slep' last night? Down by the river?"

"Yeah. I remember. Oh, sure I remember! I go there an' hide in the brush."

"Hide till I come for you. Don't let nobody see you. Hide in the brush by the river. Say that over."

"Hide in the brush by the river, down in the brush by the river."

"If you get in trouble."

"If I get in trouble."

A brake screeched outside. A call came, "Stable—Buck. Oh! Sta-able Buck."

George said, "Say it over to yourself, Lennie, so you won't forget it."

Both men glanced up, for the rectangle of sunshine in the doorway was cut off. A girl was standing there looking in. She had full, rouged lips and wide-spaced eyes, heavily made up. Her fingernails were red. Her hair hung in little rolled clusters, like sausages. She wore a cotton house dress and red mules, on the insteps of which were little bouquets of red ostrich feathers. "I'm lookin' for Curley," she said. Her voice had a nasal, brittle quality.

George looked away from her and then back. "He was in here a minute ago, but he went."

"Oh!" She put her hands behind her back and leaned against the door frame so that her body was thrown forward. "You're the new fellas that just come, ain't ya?"

"Yeah."

Lennie's eyes moved down over her body, and though she did not seem to be looking at Lennie she bridled a little. She looked at her fingernails. "Sometimes Curley's in here," she explained.

George said brusquely, "Well he ain't now."

"If he ain't, I guess I better look some place else," she said playfully.

Lennie watched her, fascinated. George said, "If I see him, I'll pass the word you was looking for him."

She smiled archly and twitched her body. "Nobody can't blame a person for lookin'," she said. There were footsteps behind her, going by. She turned her head. "Hi, Slim," she said.

Slim's voice came through the door. "Hi, Good-lookin'."

"I'm tryin' to find Curley, Slim."

"Well, you ain't tryin' very hard. I seen him goin' in your house."

She was suddenly apprehensive. " 'Bye, boys," she called into the bunk house, and she hurried away.

George looked around at Lennie. "Jesus, what a tramp," he said. "So that's what Curley picks for a wife."

"She's purty," said Lennie defensively.

"Yeah, and she's sure hidin' it. Curley got his work ahead of him. Bet she'd clear out for twenty bucks."

Lennie still stared at the doorway where she had been. "Gosh, she was purty." He smiled admiringly. George looked quickly down at him and then he took him by an ear and shook him.

"Listen to me, you crazy bastard," he said fiercely. "Don't you even take a look at that bitch. I don't care what she says and what she does. I seen 'em poison before, but I never seen no piece of jail bait worse than her. You leave her be."

Lennie tried to disengage his ear. "I never done nothing, George."

59

"No, you never. But when she was standin'
in the doorway showin' her legs, you wasn't
lookin' the other way, neither."

"I never meant no harm, George. Honest I
never."

"Well, you keep away from her, 'cause she's
a rat-trap if I ever seen one. You let Curley take
the rap. He let himself in for it. Glove fulla
vaseline," George said disgustedly. "An' I bet
he's eatin' raw eggs and writin' to the patent
medicine houses."

Lennie cried out suddenly—"I don' like this
place, George. This ain't no good place. I wanna
get outa here."

"We gotta keep it till we get a stake. We
can't help it, Lennie. We'll get out jus' as soon
as we can. I don't like it no better than you do."
He went back to the table and set out a new
solitaire hand. "No, I don't like it," he said.
"For two bits I'd shove out of here. If we can
get jus' a few dollars in the poke we'll shove off
and go up the American River and pan gold.

We can make maybe a couple of dollars a day there, and we might hit a pocket."

Lennie leaned eagerly toward him. "Le's go, George. Le's get outta here. It's mean here."

"We gotta stay," George said shortly. "Shut up now. The guys'll be comin' in."

From the washroom nearby came the sound of running water and rattling basins. George studied the cards. "Maybe we oughtta wash up," he said. "But we ain't done nothing to get dirty."

A tall man stood in the doorway. He held a crushed Stetson hat under his arm while he combed his long, black, damp hair straight back. Like the others he wore blue jeans and a short denim jacket. When he had finished combing his hair he moved into the room, and he moved with a majesty only achieved by royalty and master craftsmen. He was a jerkline skinner, the prince of the ranch, capable of driving ten, sixteen, even twenty mules with a single line to the leaders. He was capable of killing a fly on the

wheeler's butt with a bull whip without touching the mule. There was a gravity in his manner
and a quiet so profound that all talk stopped
when he spoke. His authority was so great that
his word was taken on any subject, be it politics
or love. This was Slim, the jerkline skinner. His
hatchet face was ageless. He might have been
thirty-five or fifty. His ear heard more than was
said to him, and his slow speech had overtones
not of thought, but of understanding beyond
thought. His hands, large and lean, were as deli-
cate in their action as those of a temple dancer.

He smoothed out his crushed hat, creased it in
the middle and put it on. He looked kindly at
the two in the bunk house. "It's brighter'n a
bitch outside," he said gently. "Can't hardly see
nothing in here. You the new guys?"

"Just come," said George.

"Gonna buck barley?"

"That's what the boss says."

Slim sat down on a box across the table from
George. He studied the solitaire hand that was

upside down to him. "Hope you get on my team," he said. His voice was very gentle. "I gotta pair of punks on my team that don't know a barley bag from a blue ball. You guys ever bucked any barley?"

"Hell, yes," said George. "I ain't nothing to scream about, but that big bastard there can put up more grain alone than most pairs can."

Lennie, who had been following the conversation back and forth with his eyes, smiled complacently at the compliment. Slim looked approvingly at George for having given the compliment. He leaned over the table and snapped the corner of a loose card. "You guys travel around together?" His tone was friendly. It invited confidence without demanding it.

"Sure," said George. "We kinda look after each other." He indicated Lennie with his thumb. "He ain't bright. Hell of a good worker, though. Hell of a nice fella, but he ain't bright. I've knew him for a long time."

Slim looked through George and beyond him.

63

"Ain't many guys travel around together," he mused. "I don't know why. Maybe ever'body in the whole damn world is scared of each other."

"It's a lot nicer to go around with a guy you know," said George.

A powerful, big-stomached man came into the bunk house. His head still dripped water from the scrubbing and dousing. "Hi, Slim," he said, and then stopped and stared at George and Lennie.

"These guys jus' come," said Slim by way of introduction.

"Glad ta meet ya," the big man said. "My name's Carlson."

"I'm George Milton. This here's Lennie Small."

"Glad ta meet ya," Carlson said again. "He ain't very small." He chuckled softly at his joke. "Ain't small at all," he repeated. "Meant to ask you, Slim—how's your bitch? I seen she wasn't under your wagon this morning."

"She slang her pups last night," said Slim. "Nine of 'em. I drowned four of 'em right off. She couldn't feed that many."

"Got five left, huh?"

"Yeah, five. I kept the biggest."

"What kinda dogs you think they're gonna be?"

"I dunno," said Slim. "Some kinda shepherds, I guess. That's the most kind I seen around here when she was in heat."

Carlson went on, "Got five pups, huh. Gonna keep all of 'em?"

"I dunno. Have to keep 'em a while so they can drink Lulu's milk."

Carlson said thoughtfully, "Well, looka here, Slim. I been thinkin'. That dog of Candy's is so God damn old he can't hardly walk. Stinks like hell, too. Ever' time he comes into the bunk house I can smell him for two, three days. Why'n't you get Candy to shoot his old dog and give him one of the pups to raise up? I can smell that dog a mile away. Got no teeth, damn near blind, can't eat. Candy feeds him milk. He can't chew nothing else."

George had been staring intently at Slim. Suddenly a triangle began to ring outside, slowly at first, and then faster and faster until the beat of it disappeared into one ringing sound. It stopped as suddenly as it had started.

"There she goes," said Carlson.

Outside, there was a burst of voices as a group of men went by.

Slim stood up slowly and with dignity. "You guys better come on while they's still something to eat. Won't be nothing left in a couple of minutes."

Carlson stepped back to let Slim precede him, and then the two of them went out the door.

Lennie was watching George excitedly. George rumpled his cards into a messy pile. "Yeah!" George said, "I heard him, Lennie. I'll ask him."

"A brown and white one," Lennie cried excitedly.

"Come on. Le's get dinner. I don't know whether he got a brown and white one."

Lennie didn't move from his bunk. "You ask him right away, George, so he won't kill no more of 'em."

"Sure. Come on now, get up on your feet."

Lennie rolled off his bunk and stood up, and the two of them started for the door. Just as they reached it, Curley bounced in.

"You seen a girl around here?" he demanded angrily.

George said coldly. " 'Bout half an hour ago maybe."

"Well what the hell was she doin'?"

George stood still, watching the angry little man. He said insultingly, "She said—she was lookin' for you."

Curley seemed really to see George for the first time. His eyes flashed over George, took in his height, measured his reach, looked at his trim middle. "Well, which way'd she go?" he demanded at last.

"I dunno," said George. "I didn' watch her go."

Curley scowled at him, and turning, hurried out the door.

George said, "Ya know, Lennie, I'm scared I'm gonna tangle with that bastard myself. I hate his guts. Jesus Christ! Come on. They won't be a damn thing left to eat."

They went out the door. The sunshine lay in a thin line under the window. From a distance there could be heard a rattle of dishes.

After a moment the ancient dog walked lamely in through the open door. He gazed about with mild, half-blind eyes. He sniffed, and then lay down and put his head between his paws. Curley popped into the doorway again and stood looking into the room. The dog raised his head, but when Curley jerked out, the grizzled head sank to the floor again.

3

ALTHOUGH there was evening brightness showing through the windows of the bunk house, inside it was dusk. Through the open door came the thuds and occasional clangs of a horseshoe game, and now and then the sound of voices raised in approval or derision.

Slim and George came into the darkening bunkhouse together. Slim reached up over the card table and turned on the tin-shaded electric light. Instantly the table was brilliant with light, and the cone of the shade threw its brightness straight downward, leaving the corners of the bunk house still in dusk. Slim sat down on a box and George took his place opposite.

"It wasn't nothing," said Slim. "I would of had to drowned most of 'em anyways. No need to thank me about that."

George said, "It wasn't much to you, maybe, but it was a hell of a lot to him. Jesus Christ, I don't know how we're gonna get him to sleep in here. He'll want to sleep right out in the barn with 'em. We'll have trouble keepin' him from getting right in the box with them pups."

"It wasn't nothing," Slim repeated. "Say, you sure was right about him. Maybe he ain't bright, but I never seen such a worker. He damn near killed his partner buckin' barley. There ain't nobody can keep up with him. God awmighty I never seen such a strong guy."

George spoke proudly. "Jus' tell Lennie what to do an' he'll do it if it don't take no figuring. He can't think of nothing to do himself, but he sure can take orders."

There was a clang of horseshoe on iron stake outside and a little cheer of voices.

Slim moved back slightly so the light was not on his face. "Funny how you an' him string along together." It was Slim's calm invitation to confidence.

"What's funny about it?" George demanded defensively.

"Oh, I dunno. Hardly none of the guys ever travel together. I hardly never seen two guys travel together. You know how the hands are, they just come in and get their bunk and work a month, and then they quit and go out alone. Never seem to give a damn about nobody. It jus' seems kinda funny a cuckoo like him and a smart little guy like you travelin' together."

"He ain't no cuckoo," said George. "He's dumb as hell, but he ain't crazy. An' I ain't so bright neither, or I wouldn't be buckin' barley for my fifty and found. If I was bright, if I was even a little bit smart, I'd have my own little place, an' I'd be bringin' in my own crops, 'stead of doin' all the work and not getting what comes up outa the ground." George fell silent. He wanted to talk. Slim neither encouraged nor discouraged him. He just sat back quiet and receptive.

"It ain't so funny, him an' me goin' aroun' together," George said at last. "Him and me was both born in Auburn. I knowed his Aunt Clara. She took him when he was a baby and raised him up. When his Aunt Clara died, Lennie just come along with me out workin'. Got kinda used to each other after a little while."

"Umm," said Slim.

George looked over at Slim and saw the calm, God-like eyes fastened on him. "Funny," said George. "I used to have a hell of a lot of fun with 'im. Used to play jokes on 'im 'cause he was too dumb to take care of 'imself. But he was too dumb even to know he had a joke played on him. I had fun. Made me seem God damn smart alongside of him. Why he'd do any damn thing I tol' him. If I tol' him to walk over a cliff, over he'd go. That wasn't so damn much fun after a while. He never got mad about it, neither. I've beat the hell outa him, and he coulda bust every bone in my body jus' with his han's, but he never lifted a finger against me." George's voice was taking on the tone of confession. "Tell you what made me stop that. One day a bunch of guys was standin' around up on the Sacramento River. I was feelin' pretty smart. I turns to Lennie and says, 'Jump in.' An' he jumps. Couldn't swim a stroke. He damn near drowned before we could get him. An' he was so damn nice to me for pullin' him out. Clean forgot I told him to jump in. Well, I ain't done nothing like that no more."

"He's a nice fella," said Slim. "Guy don't need no sense to be a nice fella. Seems to me sometimes it jus' works the other way around. Take a real smart guy and he ain't hardly ever a nice fella."

George stacked the scattered cards and began to lay out his solitaire hand. The shoes thudded on the ground outside. At the windows the light of the evening still made the window squares bright.

"I ain't got no people," George said. "I seen the guys that go around on the ranches alone. That ain't no good. They don't have no fun.

After a long time they get mean. They get wantin' to fight all the time."

"Yeah, they get mean," Slim agreed. "They get so they don't want to talk to nobody."

" 'Course Lennie's a God damn nuisance most of the time," said George. "But you get used to goin' around with a guy an' you can't get rid of him."

"He ain't mean," said Slim. "I can see Lennie ain't a bit mean."

" 'Course he ain't mean. But he gets in trouble alla time because he's so God damn dumb. Like what happened in Weed——" He stopped, stopped in the middle of turning over a card. He looked alarmed and peered over at Slim. "You wouldn't tell nobody?"

"What'd he do in Weed?" Slim asked calmly.

"You wouldn' tell? . . . . No, 'course you wouldn'."

"What'd he do in Weed?" Slim asked again.

"Well, he seen this girl in a red dress. Dumb bastard like he is, he wants to touch ever'thing he likes. Just wants to feel it. So he reaches out to feel this red dress an' the girl lets out a squawk, and that gets Lennie all mixed up, and he holds on 'cause that's the only thing he can think to do. Well, this girl squawks and squawks. I was jus' a little bit off, and I heard all the yellin', so I comes running, an' by that time Lennie's so scared all he can think to do is jus' hold on. I socked him over the head with a fence picket to make him let go. He was so scairt he couldn't let go of that dress. And he's so God damn strong, you know."

Slim's eyes were level and unwinking. He nodded very slowly. "So what happens?"

George carefully built his line of solitaire cards. "Well, that girl rabbits in an' tells the law she been raped. The guys in Weed start a party out to lynch Lennie. So we sit in a irrigation ditch under water all the rest of that day. Got on'y our heads sticking outa water, an' up under the grass that sticks out from the side of the ditch. An' that night we scrammed outa there."

75

Slim sat in silence for a moment. "Didn't hurt the girl none, huh?" he asked finally.

"Hell, no. He just scared her. I'd be scared too if he grabbed me. But he never hurt her. He jus' wanted to touch that red dress, like he wants to pet them pups all the time."

"He ain't mean," said Slim. "I can tell a mean guy a mile off."

" 'Course he ain't, and he'll do any damn thing I——"

Lennie came in through the door. He wore his blue denim coat over his shoulders like a cape, and he walked hunched way over.

"Hi, Lennie," said George. "How you like the pup now?"

Lennie said breathlessly, "He's brown an' white jus' like I wanted." He went directly to his bunk and lay down and turned his face to the wall and drew up his knees.

George put down his cards very deliberately. "Lennie," he said sharply.

Lennie twisted his neck and looked over his shoulder. "Huh? What you want, George?"

"I tol' you you couldn't bring that pup in here."

"What pup, George? I ain't got no pup."

George went quickly to him, grabbed him by the shoulder and rolled him over. He reached down and picked the tiny puppy from where Lennie had been concealing it against his stomach.

Lennie sat up quickly. "Give 'um to me, George."

George said, "You get right up an' take this pup back to the nest. He's gotta sleep with his mother. You want to kill him? Just born last night an' you take him out of the nest. You take him back or I'll tell Slim not to let you have him."

Lennie held out his hands pleadingly. "Give 'um to me, George. I'll take 'um back. I didn't mean no harm, George. Honest I didn't. I jus' wanted to pet 'um a little."

George handed the pup to him. "Awright. You get him back there quick, and don't you

77

take him out no more. You'll kill him, the first thing you know." Lennie fairly scuttled out of the room.

Slim had not moved. His calm eyes followed Lennie out the door. "Jesus," he said. "He's jes' like a kid, ain't he."

"Sure he's jes' like a kid. There ain't no more harm in him than a kid neither, except he's so strong. I bet he won't come in here to sleep to-night. He'd sleep right alongside that box in the barn. Well—let 'im. He ain't doin' no harm out there."

It was almost dark outside now. Old Candy, the swamper, came in and went to his bunk, and behind him struggled his old dog. "Hello, Slim. Hello, George. Didn't neither of you play horse-shoes?"

"I don't like to play ever' night," said Slim.

Candy went on, "Either you guys got a slug of whisky? I gotta gut ache."

"I ain't," said Slim. "I'd drink it myself if I had, an' I ain't got a gut ache neither."

"Gotta bad gut ache," said Candy. "Them God damn turnips give it to me. I knowed they was going to before I ever eat 'em."

The thick-bodied Carlson came in out of the darkening yard. He walked to the other end of the bunk house and turned on the second shaded light. "Darker'n hell in here," he said. "Jesus, how that nigger can pitch shoes."

"He's plenty good," said Slim.

"Damn right he is," said Carlson. "He don't give nobody else a chance to win——" He stopped and sniffed the air, and still sniffing, looked down at the old dog. "God awmighty, that dog stinks. Get him outa here, Candy! I don't know nothing that stinks as bad as an old dog. You gotta get him out."

Candy rolled to the edge of his bunk. He reached over and patted the ancient dog, and he apologized, "I been around him so much I never notice how he stinks."

"Well, I can't stand him in here," said Carlson. "That stink hangs around even after he's gone. He walked over with his heavy-legged stride and looked down at the dog. "Got no teeth," he said. "He's all stiff with rheumatism. He ain't no good to you, Candy. An' he ain't no good to himself. Why'n't you shoot him, Candy?"

The old man squirmed uncomfortably. "Well —hell! I had him so long. Had him since he was a pup. I herded sheep with him." He said proudly, "You wouldn't think it to look at him now, but he was the best damn sheep dog I ever seen."

George said, "I seen a guy in Weed that had an Airedale could herd sheep. Learned it from the other dogs."

Carlson was not to be put off. "Look, Candy. This ol' dog jus' suffers hisself all the time. If you was to take him out and shoot him right in the back of the head—" he leaned over and pointed, "—right there, why he'd never know what hit him."

Candy looked about unhappily. "No," he said

softly. "No, I couldn' do that. I had 'im too long."

"He don't have no fun," Carlson insisted. "And he stinks to beat hell. Tell you what. I'll shoot him for you. Then it won't be you that does it."

Candy threw his legs off his bunk. He scratched the white stubble whiskers on his cheek nervously. "I'm so used to him," he said softly. "I had him from a pup."

"Well, you ain't bein' kind to him keepin' him alive," said Carlson. "Look, Slim's bitch got a litter right now. I bet Slim would give you one of them pups to raise up, wouldn't you, Slim?"

The skinner had been studying the old dog with his calm eyes. "Yeah," he said. "You can have a pup if you want to." He seemed to shake himself free for speech. "Carl's right, Candy. That dog ain't no good to himself. I wisht somebody'd shoot me if I get old an' a cripple."

Candy looked helplessly at him, for Slim's opinions were law. "Maybe it'd hurt him," he suggested. "I don't mind takin' care of him."

Carlson said, "The way I'd shoot him, he wouldn't feel nothing. I'd put the gun right there." He pointed with his toe. "Right back of the head. He wouldn't even quiver."

Candy looked for help from face to face. It was quite dark outside by now. A young laboring man came in. His sloping shoulders were bent forward and he walked heavily on his heels, as though he carried the invisible grain bag. He went to his bunk and put his hat on his shelf. Then he picked a pulp magazine from his shelf and brought it to the light over the table. "Did I show you this, Slim?" he asked.

"Show me what?"

The young man turned to the back of the magazine, put it down on the table and pointed with his finger. "Right there, read that." Slim bent over it. "Go on," said the young man. "Read it out loud."

" 'Dear Editor' ": Slim read slowly. " 'I read your mag for six years and I think it is the best

82

on the market. I like stories by Peter Rand. I think he is a whing-ding. Give us more like the Dark Rider. I don't write many letters. Just thought I would tell you I think your mag is the best dime's worth I ever spent.' "

Slim looked up questioningly. "What you want me to read that for?"

Whit said, "Go on. Read the name at the bottom."

Slim read, " 'Yours for success, William Tenner.' " He glanced up at Whit again. "What you want me to read that for?"

Whit closed the magazine impressively. "Don't you remember Bill Tenner? Worked here about three months ago?"

Slim thought. . . . "Little guy?" he asked. "Drove a cultivator?"

"That's him," Whit cried. "That's the guy!"

"You think he's the guy wrote this letter?"

"I know it. Bill and me was in here one day. Bill had one of them books that just come. He was lookin' in it and he says, 'I wrote a letter.

83

Wonder if they put it in the book!' But it wasn't there. Bill says, 'Maybe they're savin' it for later.' An' that's just what they done. There it is."

"Guess you're right," said Slim. "Got it right in the book."

George held out his hand for the magazine. "Let's look at it?"

Whit found the place again, but he did not surrender his hold on it. He pointed out the letter with his forefinger. And then he went to his box shelf and laid the magazine carefully in. "I wonder if Bill seen it," he said. "Bill and me worked in that patch of field peas. Run cultivators, both of us. Bill was a hell of a nice fella."

During the conversation Carlson had refused to be drawn in. He continued to look down at the old dog. Candy watched him uneasily. At last Carlson said, "If you want me to, I'll put the old devil out of his misery right now and get it over with. Ain't nothing left for him. Can't eat, can't see, can't even walk without hurtin'."

Candy said hopefully, "You ain't got no gun."

"The hell I ain't. Got a Luger. It won't hurt him none at all."

Candy said, "Maybe tomorra. Le's wait till tomorra."

"I don't see no reason for it," said Carlson. He went to his bunk, pulled his bag from underneath it and took out a Luger pistol. "Le's get it over with," he said. "We can't sleep with him stinkin' around in here." He put the pistol in his hip pocket.

Candy looked a long time at Slim to try to find some reversal. And Slim gave him none. At last Candy said softly and hopelessly, "Awright —take 'im." He did not look down at the dog at all. He lay back on his bunk and crossed his arms behind his head and stared at the ceiling.

From his pocket Carlson took a little leather thong. He stooped over and tied it around the old dog's neck. All the men except Candy watched him. "Come boy. Come on, boy," he said gently. And he said apologetically to Candy, "He won't even feel it." Candy did not move nor answer him. He twitched the thong. "Come on, boy." The old dog got slowly and stiffly to his feet and followed the gently pulling leash.

Slim said, "Carlson."

"Yeah?"

"You know what to do."

"What ya mean, Slim?"

"Take a shovel," said Slim shortly.

"Oh, sure! I get you." He led the dog out into the darkness.

George followed to the door and shut the door and set the latch gently in its place. Candy lay rigidly on his bed staring at the ceiling.

Slim said loudly, "One of my lead mules got a bad hoof. Got to get some tar on it." His voice trailed off. It was silent outside. Carlson's footsteps died away. The silence come into the room. And the silence lasted.

George chuckled, "I bet Lennie's right out there in the barn with his pup. He won't want to come in here no more now he's got a pup."

Slim said, "Candy, you can have any one of them pups you want."

Candy did not answer. The silence fell on the room again. It came out of the night and invaded the room. George said, "Anybody like to play a little euchre?"

"I'll play out a few with you," said Whit.

They took places opposite each other at the table under the light, but George did not shuffle the cards. He rippled the edge of the deck nervously, and the little snapping noise drew the eyes of all the men in the room, so that he stopped doing it. The silence fell on the room again. A minute passed, and another minute. Candy lay still, staring at the ceiling. Slim gazed at him for a moment and then looked down at his hands; he subdued one hand with the other, and held it down. There came a little gnawing sound from under the floor and all the men looked down toward it gratefully. Only Candy continued to stare at the ceiling.

"Sounds like there was a rat under there," said George. "We ought to get a trap down there."

Whit broke out, "What the hell's takin' him so long? Lay out some cards, why don't you? We ain't going to get no euchre played this way."

George brought the cards together tightly and studied the backs of them. The silence was in the room again.

A shot sounded in the distance. The men looked quickly at the old man. Every head turned toward him.

For a moment he continued to stare at the ceiling. Then he rolled slowly over and faced the wall and lay silent.

George shuffled the cards noisily and dealt them. Whit drew a scoring board to him and set the pegs to start. Whit said, "I guess you guys really come here to work."

"How do ya mean?" George asked.

Whit laughed. "Well, ya come on a Friday. You got two days to work till Sunday."

"I don't see how you figure," said George.

Whit laughed again. "You do if you been

around these big ranches much. Guy that wants to look over a ranch comes in Sat'day afternoon. He gets Sat'day night supper an' three meals on Sunday, and he can quit Monday mornin' after breakfast without turning his hand. But you come to work Friday noon. You got to put in a day an' a half no matter how you figure."

George looked at him levelly. "We're gonna stick aroun' a while," he said. "Me an' Lennie's gonna roll up a stake."

The door opened quietly and the stable buck put in his head; a lean negro head, lined with pain, the eyes patient. "Mr. Slim."

Slim took his eyes from old Candy. "Huh? Oh! Hello, Crooks. What's'a matter?"

"You told me to warm up tar for that mule's foot. I got it warm."

"Oh! Sure, Crooks. I'll come right out an' put it on."

"I can do it if you want, Mr. Slim."

"No. I'll come do it myself." He stood up. Crooks said, "Mr. Slim."

"Yeah."

"That big new guy's messin' around **your** pups out in the barn."

"Well, he ain't doin' no harm. I give him **one of** them pups."

"Just thought I'd tell ya," said Crooks. "He's takin' 'em outa the nest and handlin' them. That won't do them no good."

"He won't hurt 'em," said Slim. "I'll come along with you now."

George looked up. "If that crazy bastard's foolin' around too much, jus' kick him out, Slim."

Slim followed the stable buck out of the room.

George dealt and Whit picked up his cards and examined them. "Seen the new kid yet?" he asked.

"What kid?" George asked.

"Why, Curley's new wife."

"Yeah, I seen her."

"Well, ain't she a looloo?"

"I ain't seen that much of her," said George.

Whit laid down his cards impressively. "Well, stick around an' keep your eyes open. You'll see plenty. She ain't concealin' nothing. I never seen nobody like her. She got the eye goin' all the time on everybody. I bet she even gives the stable buck the eye. I don't know what the hell she wants."

George asked casually, "Been any trouble since she got here?"

It was obvious that Whit was not interested in his cards. He laid his hand down and George scooped it in. George laid out his deliberate solitaire hand—seven cards, and six on top, and five on top of those.

Whit said, "I see what you mean. No, they ain't been nothing yet. Curley's got yella-jackets in his drawers, but that's all so far. Ever' time the guys is around she shows up. She's lookin' for Curley, or she thought she lef' somethin' layin' around and she's lookin' for it. Seems like she can't keep away from guys. An' Curley's pants is just crawlin' with ants, but they ain't nothing come of it yet."

George said, "She's gonna make a mess. They's gonna be a bad mess about her. She's a jail bait all set on the trigger. That Curley got his work cut out for him. Ranch with a bunch of guys on it ain't no place for a girl, specially like her."

Whit said, "If you got idears, you ought ta come in town with us guys tomorra night."

"Why? What's doin'?"

"Jus' the usual thing. We go in to old Susy's place. Hell of a nice place. Old Susy's a laugh— always crackin' jokes. Like she says when we come up on the front porch las' Sat'day night. Susy opens the door and then she yells over her shoulder, 'Get yor coats on, girls, here comes the sheriff.' She never talks dirty, neither. Got five girls there."

"What's it set you back?" George asked.

"Two an' a half. You can get a shot for two bits. Susy got nice chairs to set in, too. If a guy don't want a flop, why he can just set in the chairs and have a couple or three shots and pass the time of day and Susy don't give a damn. She ain't rushin' guys through and kickin' 'em out if they don't want a flop."

"Might go in and look the joint over," said George.

"Sure. Come along. It's a hell of a lot of fun— her crackin' jokes all the time. Like she says one time, she says, 'I've knew people that if they got a rag rug on the floor an' a kewpie doll lamp on the phonograph they think they're running a parlor house.' That's Clara's house she's talkin' about. An' Susy says, 'I know what you boys want,' she says. 'My girls is clean,' she says, 'an' there ain't no water in my whisky,' she says. 'If any you guys wanta look at a kewpie doll lamp an' take your own chance gettin' burned, why you know where to go.' An' she says, 'There's guys around here walkin' bow-legged 'cause they like to look at a kewpie doll lamp.'"

George asked, "Clara runs the other house, huh?"

"Yeah," said Whit. "We don't never go there. Clara gets three bucks a crack and thirty-five cents a shot, and she don't crack no jokes. But Susy's place is clean and she got nice chairs. Don't let no goo-goos in, neither."

"Me an' Lennie's rollin' up a stake," said George. "I might go in an' set and have a shot, but I ain't puttin' out no two and a half."

"Well, a guy got to have some fun some-time," said Whit.

The door opened and Lennie and Carlson came in together. Lennie crept to his bunk and sat down, trying not to attract attention. Carlson reached under his bunk and brought out his bag. He didn't look at old Candy, who still faced the wall. Carlson found a little cleaning rod in the bag and a can of oil. He laid them on his bed and then brought out the pistol, took out the magazine and snapped the loaded shell from the chamber. Then he fell to cleaning the barrel with the little rod. When the ejector snapped, Candy turned over and looked for a moment at the gun before he turned back to the wall again.

Carlson said casually, "Curley been in yet?"

"No," said Whit. "What's eatin' on Curley?"

Carlson squinted down the barrel of his gun. "Lookin' for his old lady. I seen him going round and round outside."

Whit said sarcastically, "He spends half his time lookin' for her, and the rest of the time she's lookin' for him."

Curley burst into the room excitedly. "Any you guys seen my wife?" he demanded.

"She ain't been here," said Whit.

Curley looked threateningly about the room. "Where the hell's Slim?"

"Went out in the barn," said George. "He was gonna put some tar on a split hoof."

Curley's shoulders dropped and squared. "How long ago'd he go?"

"Five—ten minutes."

Curley jumped out the door and banged it after him.

Whit stood up. "I guess maybe I'd like to see this," he said. "Curley's just spoilin' or he wouldn't start for Slim. An' Curley's handy, God damn handy. Got in the finals for the Golden Gloves. He got newspaper clippings about it." He considered. "But jus' the same, he better leave Slim alone. Nobody don't know what Slim can do."

"Thinks Slim's with his wife, don't he?" said George.

"Looks like it," Whit said. " 'Course Slim ain't. Least I don't think Slim is. But I like to see the fuss if it comes off. Come on, le's go."

George said, "I'm stayin' right here. I don't want to get mixed up in nothing. Lennie and me got to make a stake."

Carlson finished the cleaning of the gun and put it in the bag and pushed the bag under his bunk. "I guess I'll go out and look her over," he said. Old Candy lay still, and Lennie, from his bunk, watched George cautiously.

When Whit and Carlson were gone and the

door closed after them, George turned to Lennie. "What you got on your mind?"

"I ain't done nothing, George. Slim says I better not pet them pups so much for a while. Slim says it ain't good for them; so I come right in. I been good, George."

"I coulda told you that," said George.

"Well, I wasn't hurtin' 'em none. I jus' had mine in my lap pettin' it."

George asked, "Did you see Slim out in the barn?"

"Sure I did. He tol' me I better not pet that pup no more."

"Did you see that girl?"

"You mean Curley's girl?"

"Yeah. Did she come in the barn?"

"No. Anyways I never seen her."

"You never seen Slim talkin' to her?"

"Uh-uh. She ain't been in the barn."

"O.K.," said George. "I guess them guys ain't gonna see no fight. If there's any fightin', Lennie, you keep out of it."

97

"I don't want no fights," said Lennie. He got up from his bunk and sat down at the table, across from George. Almost automatically George shuffled the cards and laid out his solitaire hand. He used a deliberate, thoughtful, slowness.

Lennie reached for a face card and studied it, then turned it upside down and studied it. "Both ends the same," he said. "George, why is it both end's the same?"

"I don't know," said George. "That's jus' the way they make 'em. What was Slim doin' in the barn when you seen him?"

"Slim?"

"Sure. You seen him in the barn, an' he tol' you not to pet the pups so much."

"Oh, yeah. He had a can a' tar an' a paint brush. I don't know what for."

"You sure that girl didn't come in like she come in here today?"

"No. She never come."

George sighed. "You give me a good whore

house every time," he said. "A guy can go in an' get drunk and get ever'thing outa his system all at once, an' no messes. And he knows how much it's gonna set him back. These here jail baits is just set on the trigger of the hoosegow."

Lennie followed his words admiringly, and moved his lips a little to keep up. George continued, "You remember Andy Cushman, Lennie? Went to grammar school?"

"The one that his old lady used to make hot cakes for the kids?" Lennie asked.

"Yeah. That's the one. You can remember anything if there's anything to eat in it." George looked carefully at the solitaire hand. He put an ace up on his scoring rack and piled a two, three and four of diamonds on it. "Andy's in San Quentin right now on account of a tart," said George.

Lennie drummed on the table with his fingers. "George?"

"Huh?"

"George, how long's it gonna be till we get

99

that little place an' live on the fatta the lan—an' rabbits?"

"I don' know," said George. "We gotta get a big stake together. I know a little place we can get cheap, but they ain't givin' it away."

Old Candy turned slowly over. His eyes were wide open. He watched George carefully.

Lennie said, "Tell about that place, George."

"I jus' tol' you, jus' las' night."

"Go on—tell again, George."

"Well, it's ten acres," said George. "Got a little win'mill. Got a little shack on it, an' a chicken run. Got a kitchen, orchard, cherries, apples, peaches, 'cots, nuts, got a few berries. They's a place for alfalfa and plenty water to flood it. They's a pig pen——"

"An' rabbits, George."

"No place for rabbits now, but I could easy build a few hutches and you could feed alfalfa to the rabbits."

"Damn right, I could," said Lennie. "You God damn right I could."

George's hands stopped working with the cards. His voice was growing warmer. "An' we could have a few pigs. I could build a smoke house like the one gran'pa had, an' when we kill a pig we can smoke the bacon and the hams, and make sausage an' all like that. An' when the salmon run up river we could catch a hundred of 'em an' salt 'em down or smoke 'em. We could have them for breakfast. They ain't nothing so nice as smoked salmon. When the fruit come in we could can it—and tomatoes, they're easy to can. Ever' Sunday we'd kill a chicken or a rabbit. Maybe we'd have a cow or a goat, and the cream is so God damn thick you got to cut it with a knife and take it out with a spoon."

Lennie watched him with wide eyes, and old Candy watched him too. Lennie said softly, "We could live offa the fatta the lan'."

"Sure," said George. "All kin's a vegetables in the garden, and if we want a little whisky we can sell a few eggs or something, or some milk. We'd jus' live there. We'd belong there.

There wouldn't be no more runnin' round the country and gettin' fed by a Jap cook. No, sir, we'd have our own place where we belonged and not sleep in no bunk house."

"Tell about the house, George," Lennie begged.

"Sure, we'd have a little house an' a room to ourself. Little fat iron stove, an' in the winter we'd keep a fire goin' in it. It ain't enough land so we'd have to work too hard. Maybe six, seven hours a day. We wouldn't have to buck no barley eleven hours a day. An' when we put in a crop, why, we'd be there to take the crop up. We'd know what come of our planting."

"An' rabbits," Lennie said eagerly. "An' I'd take care of 'em. Tell how I'd do that, George."

"Sure, you'd go out in the alfalfa patch an' you'd have a sack. You'd fill up the sack and bring it in an' put it in the rabbit cages."

"They'd nibble an' they'd nibble," said Lennie, "the way they do. I seen 'em."

"Ever' six weeks or so," George continued,

"them does would throw a litter so we'd have plenty rabbits to eat an' to sell. An' we'd keep a few pigeons to go flyin' around the win'mill like they done when I was a kid." He looked raptly at the wall over Lennie's head. "An' it'd be our own, an' nobody could can us. If we don't like a guy we can say, 'Get the hell out,' and by God he's got to do it. An' if a fren' come along, why we'd have an extra bunk, an' we'd say, 'Why don't you spen' the night?' an' by God he would. We'd have a setter dog and a couple stripe cats, but you gotta watch out them cats don't get the little rabbits."

Lennie breathed hard. "You jus' let 'em try to get the rabbits. I'll break their God damn necks. I'll . . . . I'll smash 'em with a stick." He subsided, grumbling to himself, threatening the future cats which might dare to disturb the future rabbits.

George sat entranced with his own picture.

When Candy spoke they both jumped as

103

though they had been caught doing something reprehensible. Candy said, "You know where's a place like that?"

George was on guard immediately. "S'pose I do," he said. "What's that to you?"

"You don't need to tell me where it's at. Might be any place."

"Sure," said George. "That's right. You couldn't find it in a hundred years."

Candy went on excitedly, "How much they want for a place like that?"

George watched him suspiciously. "Well—I could get it for six hundred bucks. The ol' people that owns it is flat bust an' the ol' lady needs an operation. Say—what's it to you? You got nothing to do with us."

Candy said, "I ain't much good with on'y one hand. I lost my hand right here on this ranch. That's why they give me a job swampin'. An' they give me two hunderd an' fifty dollars 'cause I los' my hand. An' I got fifty more saved up right in the bank, right now. Tha's three hunderd, and I got fifty more comin' the end a the month. Tell you what——" He leaned forward eagerly. "S'pose I went in with you guys. Tha's three hunderd an' fifty bucks I'd put in. I ain't much good, but I could cook and tend the chickens and hoe the garden some. How'd that be?"

George half-closed his eyes. "I gotta think about that. We was always gonna do it by ourselves."

Candy interrupted him, "I'd make a will an' leave my share to you guys in case I kick off, 'cause I ain't got no relatives nor nothing. You guys got any money? Maybe we could do her right now?"

George spat on the floor disgustedly. "We got ten bucks between us." Then he said thoughtfully, "Look, if me an' Lennie work a month an' don't spen' nothing, we'll have a hunderd bucks. That'd be four fifty. I bet we could swing her for that. Then you an' Lennie could go get her started an' I'd get a job an' make up the res', an' you could sell eggs an' stuff like that."

They fell into a silence. They looked at one another, amazed. This thing they had never really believed in was coming true. George said reverently, "Jesus Christ! I bet we could swing her." His eyes were full of wonder. "I bet we could swing her," he repeated softly.

Candy sat on the edge of his bunk. He scratched the stump of his wrist nervously. "I got hurt four year ago," he said. "They'll can me purty soon. Jus' as soon as I can't swamp out no bunk houses they'll put me on the county. Maybe if I give you guys my money, you'll let me hoe in the garden even after I ain't no good at it. An' I'll wash dishes an' little chicken stuff like that. But I'll be on our own place, an' I'll be let to work on our own place." He said miserably, "You seen what they done to my dog tonight? They says he wasn't no good to himself nor nobody else. When they can me here I wisht somebody'd shoot me. But they won't do nothing like that. I won't have no place to go, an' I can't get no more jobs. I'll have thirty dollars more comin', time you guys is ready to quit."

George stood up. "We'll do her," he said. "We'll fix up that little old place an' we'll go live there." He sat down again. They all sat still, all bemused by the beauty of the thing, each mind was popped into the future when this lovely thing should come about.

George said wonderingly, "S'pose they was a carnival or a circus come to town, or a ball game, or any damn thing." Old Candy nodded in appreciation of the idea. "We'd just go to her," George said. "We wouldn't ask nobody if we could. Jus' say, 'We'll go to her,' an' we would. Jus' milk the cow and sling some grain to the chickens an' go to her."

"An' put some grass to the rabbits," Lennie broke in. "I wouldn't never forget to feed them. When we gon'ta do it, George?"

"In one month. Right squack in one month. Know what I'm gon'ta do? I'm gon'ta write to them old people that owns the place that we'll take it. An' Candy'll send a hunderd dollars to bind her."

"Sure will," said Candy. "They got a good stove there?"

"Sure, got a nice stove, burns coal or wood."

"I'm gonna take my pup," said Lennie. "I bet by Christ he likes it there, by Jesus."

Voices were approaching from outside. George said quickly, "Don't tell nobody about it. Jus' us three an' nobody else. They li'ble to can us so we can't make no stake. Jus' go on like we was gonna buck barley the rest of our lives, then all of a sudden some day we'll go get our pay an' scram outa here."

Lennie and Candy nodded, and they were grinning with delight. "Don't tell nobody," Lennie said to himself.

Candy said, "George."

"Huh?"

"I ought to of shot that dog myself, George. I shouldn't ought to of let no stranger shoot my dog."

The door opened. Slim came in, followed by Curley and Carlson and Whit. Slim's hands were black with tar and he was scowling. Curley hung close to his elbow.

Curley said, "Well, I didn't mean nothing, Slim. I just ast you."

Slim said, "Well, you been askin' me too often. I'm gettin' God damn sick of it. If you can't look after your own God damn wife, what you expect me to do about it? You lay offa me."

"I'm jus' tryin' to tell you I didn't mean nothing," said Curley. "I jus' thought you might of saw her."

"Why'n't you tell her to stay the hell home where she belongs?" said Carlson. "You let her hang around bunk houses and pretty soon you're gonna have som'pin on your hands and you won't be able to do nothing about it."

Curley whirled on Carlson. "You keep outta this les' you wanta step outside."

Carlson laughed. "You God damn punk," he

said. "You tried to throw a scare into Slim, an'
you couldn't make it stick. Slim throwed a scare
inta you. You're yella as a frog belly. I don't
care if you're the best welter in the country.
You come for me, an' I'll kick your God damn
head off."

Candy joined the attack with joy. "Glove
fulla vaseline," he said disgustedly. Curley
glared at him. His eyes slipped on past and
lighted on Lennie; and Lennie was still smiling
with delight at the memory of the ranch.

Curley stepped over to Lennie like a terrier.
"What the hell you laughin' at?"

Lennie looked blankly at him. "Huh?"

Then Curley's rage exploded. "Come on, ya
big bastard. Get up on your feet. No big son-of-
a-bitch is gonna laugh at me. I'll show ya who's
yella."

Lennie looked helplessly at George, and then
he got up and tried to retreat. Curley was bal-
anced and poised. He slashed at Lennie with his
left, and then smashed down his nose with a

right. Lennie gave a cry of terror. Blood welled from his nose. "George," he cried. "Make 'um let me alone, George." He backed until he was against the wall, and Curley followed, slugging him in the face. Lennie's hands remained at his sides; he was too frightened to defend himself.

George was on his feet yelling, "Get him, Lennie. Don't let him do it."

Lennie covered his face with his huge paws and bleated with terror. He cried, "Make 'um stop, George." Then Curley attacked his stomach and cut off his wind.

Slim jumped up. "The dirty little rat," he cried, "I'll get 'um myself."

George put out his hand and grabbed Slim. "Wait a minute," he shouted. He cupped his hands around his mouth and yelled, "Get 'im, Lennie!"

Lennie took his hands away from his face and looked about for George, and Curley slashed at his eyes. The big face was covered with blood. George yelled again, "I said get him."

Curley's fist was swinging when Lennie reached for it. The next minute Curley was flopping like a fish on a line, and his closed fist was lost in Lennie's big hand. George ran down the room. "Leggo of him, Lennie. Let go."

But Lennie watched in terror the flopping little man whom he held. Blood ran down Lennie's face, one of his eyes was cut and closed. George slapped him in the face again and again, and still Lennie held on to the closed fist. Curley was white and shrunken by now, and his struggling had become weak. He stood crying, his fist lost in Lennie's paw.

George shouted over and over, "Leggo his hand, Lennie. Leggo. Slim, come help me while the guy got any hand left."

Suddenly Lennie let go his hold. He crouched cowering against the wall. "You tol' me to, George," he said miserably.

Curley sat down on the floor, looking in wonder at his crushed hand. Slim and Carlson bent over him. Then Slim straightened up and regarded Lennie with horror. "We got to get him in to a doctor," he said. "Looks to me like ever' bone in his han' is bust."

"I didn't wanta," Lennie cried. "I didn't wanta hurt him."

Slim said, "Carlson, you get the candy wagon hitched up. We'll take 'um into Soledad an' get 'um fixed up." Carlson hurried out. Slim turned to the whimpering Lennie. "It ain't your fault," he said. "This punk sure had it comin' to him. But—Jesus! He ain't hardly got no han' left." Slim hurried out, and in a moment returned with a tin cup of water. He held it to Curley's lips.

George said, "Slim, will we get canned now? We need the stake. Will Curley's old man can us now?"

Slim smiled wryly. He knelt down beside Curley. "You got your senses in hand enough to listen?" he asked. Curley nodded. "Well, then listen," Slim went on. "I think you got your han' caught in a machine. If you don't tell nobody what happened, we ain't going to. But you jus' tell an' try to get this guy canned and we'll tell ever'body, an' then will you get the laugh."

"I won't tell," said Curley. He avoided looking at Lennie.

Buggy wheels sounded outside. Slim helped Curley up. "Come on now. Carlson's gonna take you to a doctor." He helped Curley out the door. The sound of wheels drew away. In a moment Slim came back into the bunk house. He looked at Lennie, still crouched fearfully against the wall. "Le's see your hands," he asked.

Lennie stuck out his hands.

"Christ awmighty, I hate to have you mad at me," Slim said.

George broke in, "Lennie was jus' scairt," he explained. "He didn't know what to do. I told you nobody ought never to fight him. No, I guess it was Candy I told."

Candy nodded solemnly. "That's jus' what you done," he said. "Right this morning when

Curley first lit intil your fren', you says, 'He better not fool with Lennie if he knows what's good for 'um.' That's jus' what you says to me."

George turned to Lennie. "It ain't your fault," he said. "You don't need to be scairt no more. You done jus' what I tol' you to. Maybe you better go in the wash room an' clean up your face. You look like hell."

Lennie smiled with his bruised mouth. "I didn't want no trouble," he said. He walked toward the door, but just before he came to it, he turned back. "George?"

"What you want?"

"I can still tend the rabbits, George?"

"Sure. You ain't done nothing wrong."

"I di'n't mean no harm, George."

"Well, get the hell out and wash your face."

4

CROOKS, the negro stable buck, had his bunk in the harness room; a little shed that leaned off the wall of the barn. On one side of the little room there was a square four-paned window, and on the other, a narrow plank door leading into the barn. Crooks' bunk was a long box filled with straw, on which his blankets were flung. On the wall by the window there were pegs on which hung broken harness in process of being mended; strips of new leather; and under the window itself a little bench for leather-working tools, curved knives and needles and balls of linen thread, and a small hand riveter. On pegs were also pieces of harness, a split collar with the horsehair stuffing sticking out, a broken hame, and a trace chain with its leather covering split. Crooks had his apple box over his bunk, and in it a range of medicine bottles, both for himself and for the horses. There were cans of saddle soap and a drippy can of tar with its paint brush sticking over the edge. And scattered about the floor were a number of personal possessions; for, being alone, Crooks could leave his things about, and being a stable buck and a cripple, he was more permanent than the other men, and he had accumulated more possessions than he could carry on his back.

Crooks possessed several pairs of shoes, a pair of rubber boots, a big alarm clock and a single-barreled shotgun. And he had books, too; a tattered dictionary and a mauled copy of the California civil code for 1905. There were battered magazines and a few dirty books on a special shelf over his bunk. A pair of large gold-rimmed spectacles hung from a nail on the wall above his bed.

This room was swept and fairly neat, for Crooks was a proud, aloof man. He kept his distance and demanded that other people keep theirs. His body was bent over to the left by his crooked spine, and his eyes lay deep in his head, and because of their depth seemed to glitter with intensity. His lean face was lined with deep black wrinkles, and he had thin, pain-tightened lips which were lighter than his face.

It was Saturday night. Through the open door that led into the barn came the sound of moving horses, of feet stirring, of teeth champing on hay, of the rattle of halter chains. In the stable buck's room a small electric globe threw a meager yellow light.

Crooks sat on his bunk. His shirt was out of his jeans in back. In one hand he held a bottle of liniment, and with the other he rubbed his spine. Now and then he poured a few drops of the liniment into his pink-palmed hand and reached up under his shirt to rub again. He flexed his muscles against his back and shivered.

Noiselessly Lennie appeared in the open doorway and stood there looking in, his big shoulders nearly filling the opening. For a moment Crooks did not see him, but on raising his eyes he stiffened and a scowl came on his face. His hand came out from under his shirt.

Lennie smiled helplessly in an attempt to make friends.

Crooks said sharply, "You got no right to come in my room. This here's my room. Nobody got any right in here but me."

Lennie gulped and his smile grew more fawning. "I ain't doing nothing," he said. "Just come to look at my puppy. And I seen your light," he explained.

"Well, I got a right to have a light. You go on get outta my room. I ain't wanted in the bunk house, and you ain't wanted in my room."

"Why ain't you wanted?" Lennie asked.

" 'Cause I'm black. They play cards in there, but I can't play because I'm black. They say I stink. Well, I tell you, you all of you stink to me."

Lennie flapped his big hands helplessly.

"Ever'body went into town," he said. "Slim an' George an' ever'body. George says I gotta stay here an' not get in no trouble. I seen your light."

"Well, what do you want?"

"Nothing—I seen your light. I thought I could jus' come in an' set."

Crooks stared at Lennie, and he reached behind him and took down the spectacles and adjusted them over his pink ears and stared again. "I don't know what you're doin' in the barn anyway," he complained. "You ain't no skinner. They's no call for a bucker to come into the barn at all. You ain't no skinner. You ain't got nothing to do with the horses."

"The pup," Lennie repeated. "I come to see my pup."

"Well, go see your pup, then. Don't come in a place where you're not wanted."

Lennie lost his smile. He advanced a step into the room, then remembered and backed to the door again. "I looked at 'em a little. Slim says I ain't to pet 'em very much."

Crooks said, "Well, you been takin' 'em out of the nest all the time. I wonder the old lady don't move 'em someplace else."

"Oh, she don't care. She lets me." Lennie had moved into the room again.

Crooks scowled, but Lennie's disarming smile defeated him. "Come on in and set a while," Crooks said. " 'Long as you won't get out and leave me alone, you might as well set down." His tone was a little more friendly. "All the boys gone into town, huh?"

"All but old Candy. He just sets in the bunk house sharpening his pencil and sharpening and figuring."

Crooks adjusted his glasses. "Figuring? What's Candy figuring about?"

Lennie almost shouted, " 'Bout the rabbits."

"You're nuts," said Crooks. "You're crazy as a wedge. What rabbits you talkin' about?"

"The rabbits we're gonna get, and I get to

tend 'em, cut grass an' give 'em water, an' like that."

"Jus' nuts," said Crooks. "I don't blame the guy you travel with for keepin' you outa sight."

Lennie said quietly, "It ain't no lie. We're gonna do it. Gonna get a little place an' live on the fatta the lan'."

Crooks settled himself more comfortably on his bunk. "Set down," he invited. "Set down on the nail keg."

Lennie hunched down on the little barrel. "You think it's a lie," Lennie said, "But it ain't no lie. Ever' word's the truth, an' you can ast George."

Crooks put his dark chin into his pink palm. "You travel aroun' with George, don't ya?"

"Sure. Me an' him goes ever' place together."

Crooks continued. "Sometimes he talks, and you don't know what the hell he's talkin' about. Ain't that so?" He leaned forward, boring Lennie with his deep eyes. "Ain't that so?"

"Yeah . . . . sometimes."

"Jus' talks on, an' you don't know what the hell it's all about?"

"Yeah . . . . sometimes. But . . . . not always."

Crooks leaned forward over the edge of the bunk. "I ain't a southern negro," he said. "I was born right here in California. My old man had a chicken ranch, 'bout ten acres. The white kids come to play at our place, an' sometimes I went to play with them, and some of them was pretty nice. My ol' man didn't like that. I never knew till long later why he didn't like that. But I know now." He hesitated, and when he spoke again his voice was softer. "There wasn't another colored family for miles around. And now there ain't a colored man on this ranch an' there's jus' one family in Soledad." He laughed. "If I say something, why it's just a nigger sayin' it."

Lennie asked, "How long you think it'll be before them pups will be old enough to pet?"

Crooks laughed again. "A guy can talk to you

an' be sure you won't go blabbin'. Couple of weeks an' them pups'll be all right. George knows what he's about. Jus' talks, an' you don't understand nothing." He leaned forward excitedly. "This is just a nigger talkin', an' a busted-back nigger. So it don't mean nothing, see? You couldn't remember it anyways. I seen it over an' over—a guy talkin' to another guy and it don't make no difference if he don't hear or understand. The thing is, they're talkin', or they're settin' still not talkin'. It don't make no difference, no difference." His excitement had increased until he pounded his knee with this hand. "George can tell you screwy things, and it don't matter. It's just the talking. It's just bein' with another guy. That's all." He paused.

His voice grew soft and persuasive. "S'pose George don't come back no more. S'pose he took a powder and just ain't coming back. What'll you do then?"

Lennie's attention came gradually to what had been said. "What?" he demanded.

"I said s'pose George went into town tonight and you never heard of him no more." Crooks pressed forward some kind of private victory. "Just s'pose that," he repeated.

"He won't do it," Lennie cried. "George wouldn't do nothing like that. I been with George a long time. He'll come back to-night——" But the doubt was too much for him. "Don't you think he will?"

Crooks' face lighted with pleasure in his torture. "Nobody can't tell what a guy'll do," he observed calmly. "Le's say he wants to come back and can't. S'pose he gets killed or hurt so he can't come back."

Lennie struggled to understand. "George won't do nothing like that," he repeated. "George is careful. He won't get hurt. He ain't never been hurt, 'cause he's careful."

"Well, s'pose, jus' s'pose he don't come back. What'll you do then?"

Lennie's face wrinkled with apprehension. "I don' know. Say, what you doin' anyways?" he cried. "This ain't true. George ain't got hurt."

Crooks bored in on him. "Want me ta tell ya what'll happen? They'll take ya to the booby hatch. They'll tie ya up with a collar, like a dog."

Suddenly Lennie's eyes centered and grew quiet, and mad. He stood up and walked dangerously toward Crooks. "Who hurt George?" he demanded.

Crooks saw the danger as it approached him. He edged back on his bunk to get out of the way. "I was just supposin'," he said. "George ain't hurt. He's all right. He'll be back all right."

Lennie stood over him. "What you supposin' for? Ain't nobody goin' to suppose no hurt to George."

Crooks removed his glasses and wiped his eyes with his fingers. "Jus' set down," he said. "George ain't hurt."

Lennie growled back to his seat on the nail

keg. "Ain't nobody goin' to talk no hurt to George," he grumbled.

Crooks said gently, "Maybe you can see now. You got George. You *know* he's goin' to come back. S'pose you didn't have nobody. S'pose you couldn't go into the bunk house and play rummy 'cause you was black. How'd you like that? S'pose you had to sit out here an' read books. Sure you could play horseshoes till it got dark, but then you got to read books. Books ain't no good. A guy needs somebody—to be near him." He whined, "A guy goes nuts if he ain't got nobody. Don't make no difference who the guy is, long's he's with you. I tell ya," he cried, "I tell ya a guy gets too lonely an' he gets sick."

"George gonna come back," Lennie reassured himself in a frightened voice. "Maybe George come back already. Maybe I better go see."

Crooks said, "I didn't mean to scare you. He'll come back. I was talkin' about myself. A

127

guy sets alone out here at night, maybe readin' books or thinkin' or stuff like that. Sometimes he gets thinkin', an' he got nothing to tell him what's so an' what ain't so. Maybe if he sees somethin', he don't know whether it's right or not. He can't turn to some other guy and ast him if he sees it too. He can't tell. He got nothing to measure by. I seen things out here. 1 wasn't drunk. I don't know if I was asleep. If some guy was with me, he could tell me I was asleep, an' then it would be all right. But I jus' don't know." Crooks was looking across the room now, looking toward the window.

Lennie said miserably, "George wun't go away and leave me. I know George wun't do that."

The stable buck went on dreamily, "I remember when I was a little kid on my old man's chicken ranch. Had two brothers. They was always near me, always there. Used to sleep right in the same room, right in the same bed—all three. Had a strawberry patch. Had an alfalfa patch. Used to turn the chickens out in the alfalfa on a sunny morning. My brothers'd set on a fence rail an' watch 'em—white chickens they was."

Gradually Lennie's interest came around to what was being said. "George says we're gonna have alfalfa for the rabbits."

"What rabbits?"

"We're gonna have rabbits an' a berry patch."

"You're nuts."

"We are too. You ast George."

"You're nuts." Crooks was scornful. "I seen hunderds of men come by on the road an' on the ranches, with their bindles on their back an' that same damn thing in their heads. Hunderds of them. They come, an' they quit an' go on; an' every damn one of 'em's got a little piece of land in his head. An' never a God damn one of 'em ever gets it. Just like heaven. Ever'body wants a little piece of lan'. I read plenty of books out here. Nobody never gets to heaven, and nobody gets no land. It's just in their head. They're all the time talkin' about it, but it's jus' in their head. He paused and looked toward the open door, for the horses were moving restlessly and the halter chains clinked. A horse whinnied. "I guess somebody's out there," Crooks said. "Maybe Slim. Slim comes in sometimes two, three times a night. Slim's a real skinner. He looks out for his team." He pulled himself painfully upright and moved toward the door. "That you, Slim?" he called.

Candy's voice answered. "Slim went in town. Say, you seen Lennie?"

"Ya mean the big guy?"

"Yeah. Seen him around any place?"

"He's in here," Crooks said shortly. He went back to his bunk and lay down.

Candy stood in the doorway scratching his bald wrist and looking blindly into the lighted room. He made no attempt to enter. "Tell ya what, Lennie. I been figuring out about them rabbits."

Crooks said irritably, "You can come in if you want."

Candy seemed embarrassed. "I do' know. 'Course, if ya want me to."

"Come on in. If ever'body's comin' in, you might just as well." It was difficult for Crooks to conceal his pleasure with anger.

Candy came in, but he was still embarrassed. "You got a nice cozy little place in here," he said to Crooks. "Must be nice to have a room all to yourself this way."

"Sure," said Crooks. "And a manure pile under the window. Sure, it's swell."

Lennie broke in, "You said about them rabbits."

Candy leaned against the wall beside the broken collar while he scratched the wrist stump. "I been here a long time," he said. "An' Crooks been here a long time. This's the first time I ever been in his room."

Crooks said darkly, "Guys don't come into a colored man's room very much. Nobody been here but Slim. Slim an' the boss."

Candy quickly changed the subject. "Slim's as good a skinner as I ever seen."

Lennie leaned toward the old swamper. "About them rabbits," he insisted.

Candy smiled. "I got it figured out. We can make some money on them rabbits if we go about it right."

"But I get to tend 'em," Lennie broke in. "George says I get to tend 'em. He promised."

Crooks interrupted brutally. "You guys is just kiddin' yourself. You'll talk about it a hell of a lot, but you won't get no land. You'll be a swamper here till they take you out in a box. Hell, I seen too many guys. Lennie here'll quit an' be on the road in two, three weeks. Seems like ever' guy got land in his head."

Candy rubbed his cheek angrily. "You God damn right we're gonna do it. George says we are. We got the money right now."

"Yeah?" said Crooks. "An' where's George now? In town in a whore house. That's where your money's goin'. Jesus, I seen it happen too many times. I seen too many guys with land in their head. They never get none under their hand."

Candy cried, "Sure they all want it. Everybody wants a little bit of land, not much. Jus' som'thin' that was his. Som'thin' he could live on and there couldn't nobody throw him off of it. I never had none. I planted crops for damn near ever'body in this state, but they wasn't my crops, and when I harvested 'em, it wasn't none of my harvest. But we gonna do it now, and don't you make no mistake about that. George ain't got the money in town. That money's in the bank. Me an' Lennie an' George. We gonna have a room to ourself. We're gonna have a dog an' rabbits an' chickens. We're gonna have green corn an' maybe a cow or a goat." He stopped, overwhelmed with his picture.

Crooks asked, "You say you got the money?"

"Damn right. We got most of it. Just a little bit more to get. Have it all in one month. George got the land all picked out, too."

Crooks reached around and explored his spine with his hand. "I never seen a guy really do it," he said. "I seen guys nearly crazy with loneliness for land, but ever' time a whore house or a blackjack game took what it takes." He hesitated. " . . . . If you . . . . guys would want a hand to work for nothing—just his keep, why I'd come an' lend a hand. I ain't so crippled I can't work like a son-of-a-bitch if I want to."

"Any you boys seen Curley?"

They swung their heads toward the door. Looking in was Curley's wife. Her face was heavily made up. Her lips were slightly parted. She breathed strongly, as though she had been running.

"Curley ain't been here," Candy said sourly.

She stood still in the doorway, smiling a little at them, rubbing the nails of one hand with the thumb and forefinger of the other. And her eyes traveled from one face to another. "They left all the weak ones here," she said finally. "Think

I don't know where they all went? Even Curley. I know where they all went."

Lennie watched her, fascinated; but Candy and Crooks were scowling down away from her eyes. Candy said, "Then if you know, why you want to ast us where Curley is at?"

She regarded them amusedly. "Funny thing," she said. "If I catch any one man, and he's alone, I get along fine with him. But just let two of the guys get together an' you won't talk. Jus' nothing but mad." She dropped her fingers and put her hands on her hips. "You're all scared of each other, that's what. Ever' one of you's scared the rest is goin' to get something on you."

After a pause Crooks said, "Maybe you better go along to your own house now. We don't want no trouble."

"Well, I ain't giving you no trouble. Think I don't like to talk to somebody ever' once in a while? Think I like to stick in that house alla time?"

Candy laid the stump of his wrist on his knee and rubbed it gently with his hand. He said accusingly, "You gotta husban'. You got no call foolin' aroun' with other guys, causin' trouble."

The girl flared up. "Sure I gotta husban'. You all seen him. Swell guy, ain't he? Spends all his time sayin' what he's gonna do to guys he don't like, and he don't like nobody. Think I'm gonna stay in that two-by-four house and listen how Curley's gonna lead with his left twict, and then bring in the ol' right cross? 'One-two' he says. 'Jus the ol' one-two an' he'll go down.'" She paused and her face lost its sullenness and grew interested. "Say—what happened to Curley's han'?"

There was an embarrassed silence. Candy stole a look at Lennie. Then he coughed. "Why . . . . Curley . . . . he got his han' caught in a machine, ma'am. Bust his han'."

She watched for a moment, and then she laughed. "Baloney! What you think you're sellin' me? Curley started som'pin' he didn' finish.

Caught in a machine—baloney! Why, he ain't give nobody the good ol' one-two since he got his han' bust. Who bust him?"

Candy repeated sullenly, "Got it caught in a machine."

"Awright," she said contemptuously. "Awright, cover 'im up if ya wanta. Whatta I care? You bindle bums think you're so damn good. Whatta ya think I am, a kid? I tell ya I could of went with shows. Not jus' one, neither. An' a guy tol' me he could put me in pitchers. . . ." She was breathless with indignation. "—Sat'iday night. Ever'body out doin' som'pin'. Ever'body! An' what am I doin'? Standin' here talkin' to a bunch of bindle stiffs—a nigger an' a dum-dum and a lousy ol' sheep—an' likin' it because they ain't nobody else."

Lennie watched her, his mouth half open. Crooks had retired into the terrible protective dignity of the negro. But a change came over old Candy. He stood up suddenly and knocked his nail keg over backward. "I had enough," he said angrily. "You ain't wanted here. We told you you ain't. An' I tell ya, you got floozy idears about what us guys amounts to. You ain't got sense enough in that chicken head to even see that we ain't stiffs. S'pose you get us canned. S'pose you do. You think we'll hit the highway an' look for another lousy two-bit job like this. You don't know that we got our own ranch to go to, an' our own house. We ain't got to stay here. We gotta house and chickens an' fruit trees an' a place a hunderd time prettier than this. An' we got fren's, that's what we got. Maybe there was a time when we was scared of gettin' canned, but we ain't no more. We got our own lan', and it's ours, an' we c'n go to it."

Curley's wife laughed at him. "Baloney," she said. "I seen too many you guys. If you had two bits in the worl', why you'd be in gettin' two shots of corn with it and suckin' the bottom of the glass. I know you guys."

Candy's face had grown redder and redder, but before she was done speaking, he had con-

trol of himself. He was the master of the situa-
tion. "I might of knew," he said gently. "Maybe
you just better go along an' roll your hoop. We
ain't got nothing to say to you at all. We know
what we got, and we don't care whether you
know it or not. So maybe you better jus' scatter
along now, 'cause Curley maybe ain't gonna like
his wife out in the barn with us 'bindle stiffs.'"

She looked from one face to another, and they
were all closed against her. And she looked
longest at Lennie, until he dropped his eyes in
embarrassment. Suddenly she said, "Where'd
you get them bruises on your face?"

Lennie looked up guiltily. "Who—me?"

"Yeah, you."

Lennie looked to Candy for help, and then
he looked at his lap again. "He got his han'
caught in a machine," he said.

Curley's wife laughed. "O.K., Machine. I'll
talk to you later. I like machines."

Candy broke in. "You let this guy alone.

Don't you do no messing aroun' with him. I'm gonna tell George what you says. George won't have you messin' with Lennie."

"Who's George?" she asked. "The little guy you come with?"

Lennie smiled happily. "That's him," he said. "That's the guy, an' he's gonna let me tend the rabbits."

"Well, if that's all you want, I might get a couple rabbits myself."

Crooks stood up from his bunk and faced her. "I had enough," he said coldly. "You got no rights comin' in a colored man's room. You got no rights messing around in here at all. Now you jus' get out, an' get out quick. If you don't, I'm gonna ast the boss not to ever let you come in the barn no more."

She turned on him in scorn. "Listen, Nigger," she said. "You know what I can do to you if you open your trap?"

Crooks stared hopelessly at her, and then he sat down on his bunk and drew into himself.

She closed on him. "You know what I could do?"

Crooks seemed to grow smaller, and he pressed himself against the wall. "Yes, ma'am."

"Well, you keep your place then, Nigger. I could get you strung up on a tree so easy it ain't even funny."

Crooks had reduced himself to nothing. There was no personality, no ego—nothing to arouse either like or dislike. He said, "Yes, ma'am," and his voice was toneless.

For a moment she stood over him as though waiting for him to move so that she could whip at him again; but Crooks sat perfectly still, his eyes averted, everything that might be hurt drawn in. She turned at last to the other two.

Old Candy was watching her, fascinated. "If you was to do that, we'd tell," he said quietly. "We'd tell about you framin' Crooks."

"Tell an' be damned," she cried. "Nobody'd listen to you, an' you know it. Nobody'd listen to you."

Candy subsided. "No . . . ." he agreed. "Nobody'd listen to us."

Lennie whined, "I wisht George was here. I wisht George was here."

Candy stepped over to him. "Don't you worry none," he said. "I jus' heard the guys comin' in. George'll be in the bunk house right now, I bet." He turned to Curley's wife. "You better go home now," he said quietly. "If you go right now, we won't tell Curley you was here."

She appraised him coolly. "I ain't sure you heard nothing."

"Better not take no chances," he said. "If you ain't sure, you better take the safe way."

She turned to Lennie. "I'm glad you bust up Curley a little bit. He got it comin' to him. Sometimes I'd like to bust him myself." She slipped out the door and disappeared into the dark barn. And while she went through the barn, the halter chains rattled, and some horses snorted and some stamped their feet.

Crooks seemed to come slowly out of the layers of protection he had put on. "Was that the truth what you said about the guys come back?" he asked.

"Sure. I heard 'em."

"Well, I didn't hear nothing."

"The gate banged," Candy said, and he went on, "Jesus Christ, Curley's wife can move quiet. I guess she had a lot of practice, though."

Crooks avoided the whole subject now. "Maybe you guys better go," he said. "I ain't sure I want you in here no more. A colored man got to have some rights even if he don't like 'em."

Candy said, "That bitch didn't ought to of said that to you."

"It wasn't nothing," Crooks said dully. "You guys comin' in an' settin' made me forget. What she says is true."

The horses snorted out in the barn and the chains rang and a voice called, "Lennie. Oh, Lennie. You in the barn?"

"It's George," Lennie cried. And he answered, "Here, George. I'm right in here."

In a second George stood framed in the door, and he looked disapprovingly about. "What you doin' in Crooks' room. You hadn't ought to be here."

Crooks nodded. "I tol' 'em, but they come in anyways."

"Well, why'n't you kick 'em out?"

"I di'n't care much," said Crooks. "Lennie's a nice fella."

Now Candy aroused himself. "Oh, George! I been figurin' and figurin'. I got it doped out how we can even make some money on them rabbits."

George scowled. "I thought I tol' you not to tell nobody about that."

Candy was crestfallen. "Didn't tell nobody but Crooks."

George said, "Well you guys get outta here. Jesus, seems like I can't go away for a minute."

Candy and Lennie stood up and went toward the door. Crooks called, "Candy!"

"Huh?"

" 'Member what I said about hoein' and doin' odd jobs?"

"Yeah," said Candy. "I remember."

"Well, jus' forget it," said Crooks. "I didn' mean it. Jus' foolin'. I wouldn' want to go no place like that."

"Well, O.K., if you feel like that. Goodnight."

The three men went out of the door. As they went through the barn the horses snorted and the halter chains rattled.

Crooks sat on his bunk and looked at the door for a moment, and then he reached for the liniment bottle. He pulled out his shirt in back, poured a little liniment in his pink palm and, reaching around, he fell slowly to rubbing his back.

5

ONE end of the great barn was piled high with new hay and over the pile hung the four-taloned jackson fork suspended from its pulley. The hay came down like a mountain slope to the other end of the barn, and there was a level place as yet unfilled with the new crop. At the sides the feeding racks were visible, and between the slats the heads of horses could be seen.

It was Sunday afternoon. The resting horses nibbled the remaining wisps of hay, and they stamped their feet and they bit the wood of the mangers and rattled the halter chains. The afternoon sun sliced in through the cracks of the barn walls and lay in bright lines on the hay. There was the buzz of flies in the air, the lazy afternoon humming.

From outside came the clang of horseshoes on the playing peg and the shouts of men, playing, encouraging, jeering. But in the barn it was quiet and humming and lazy and warm.

Only Lennie was in the barn, and Lennie sat in the hay beside a packing case under a manger in the end of the barn that had not been filled with hay. Lennie sat in the hay and looked at a little dead puppy that lay in front of him. Lennie looked at it for a long time, and then he put out his huge hand and stroked it, stroked it clear from one end to the other.

And Lennie said softly to the puppy, "Why do you got to get killed? You ain't so little as mice. I didn't bounce you hard." He bent the pup's head up and looked in its face, and he said to it, "Now maybe George ain't gonna let me tend no rabbits, if he fin's out you got killed."

He scooped a little hollow and laid the puppy in it and covered it over with hay, out of sight; but he continued to stare at the mound he had made. He said, "This ain't no bad thing like

147

I got to go hide in the brush. Oh! no. This ain't. I'll tell George I foun' it dead."

He unburied the puppy and inspected it, and he stroked it from ears to tail. He went on sorrowfully, "But he'll know. George always knows. He'll say, 'You done it. Don't try to put nothing over on me.' An' he'll say, 'Now jus' for that you don't get to tend no rabbits!' "

Suddenly his anger arose. "God damn you," he cried. "Why do you got to get killed? You ain't so little as mice." He picked up the pup and hurled it from him. He turned his back on it. He sat bent over his knees and he whispered, "Now I won't get to tend the rabbits. Now he won't let me." He rocked himself back and forth in his sorrow.

From outside came the clang of horseshoes on the iron stake, and then a little chorus of cries. Lennie got up and brought the puppy back and laid it on the hay and sat down. He stroked the pup again. "You wasn't big enough," he said. "They tol' me and tol' me you wasn't. I di'n't know you'd get killed so easy." He worked his fingers on the pup's limp ear. "Maybe George won't care," he said. "This here God damn little son-of-a-bitch wasn't nothing to George."

Curley's wife came around the end of the last stall. She came very quietly, so that Lennie didn't see her. She wore her bright cotton dress and the mules with the red ostrich feathers. Her face was made up and the little sausage curls were all in place. She was quite near to him before Lennie looked up and saw her.

In a panic he shoveled hay over the puppy with his fingers. He looked sullenly up at her.

She said, "What you got there, sonny boy?"

Lennie glared at her. "George says I ain't to have nothing to do with you—talk to you or nothing."

She laughed. "George giving you orders about everything?"

Lennie looked down at the hay. "Says I can't tend no rabbits if I talk to you or anything."

She said quietly, "He's scared Curley'll get

149

mad. Well, Curley got his arm in a sling—an' if Curley gets tough, you can break his other han'. You didn't put nothing over on me about gettin' it caught in no machine."

But Lennie was not to be drawn. "No, sir. I ain't gonna talk to you or nothing."

She knelt in the hay beside him. "Listen," she said. "All the guys got a horseshoe tenement goin' on. It's on'y about four o'clock. None of them guys is goin' to leave that tenement. Why can't I talk to you? I never get to talk to nobody. I get awful lonely."

Lennie said, "Well, I ain't supposed to talk to you or nothing."

"I get lonely," she said. "You can talk to people, but I can't talk to nobody but Curley. Else he gets mad. How'd you like not to talk to anybody?"

Lennie said, "Well, I ain't supposed to. George's scared I'll get in trouble."

She changed the subject. "What you got covered up there?"

Then all of Lennie's woe came back on him. "Jus' my pup," he said sadly. "Jus' my little pup." And he swept the hay from on top of it.

"Why, he's dead," she cried.

"He was so little," said Lennie. "I was jus' playin' with him . . . . an' he made like he's gonna bite me . . . . an' I made like I was gonna smack him . . . . an' . . . . an' I done it. An' then he was dead."

She consoled him. "Don't you worry none. He was jus' a mutt. You can get another one easy. The whole country is fulla mutts."

"It ain't that so much," Lennie explained miserably. "George ain't gonna let me tend no rabbits now."

"Why don't he?"

"Well, he said if I done any more bad things he ain't gonna let me tend the rabbits."

She moved closer to him and she spoke soothingly. "Don't you worry about talkin' to me. Listen to the guys yell out there. They got four dollars bet in that tenement. None of them ain't gonna leave till it's over."

"If George sees me talkin' to you he'll give me hell," Lennie said cautiously. "He tol' me so."

Her face grew angry. "Wha's the matter with me?" she cried. "Ain't I got a right to talk to nobody? Whatta they think I am, anyways? You're a nice guy. I don't know why I can't talk to you. I ain't doin' no harm to you."

"Well, George says you'll get us in a mess."

"Aw, nuts!" she said. "What kinda harm am I doin' to you? Seems like they ain't none of them cares how I gotta live. I tell you I ain't used to livin' like this. I coulda made somethin' of myself." She said darkly, "Maybe I will yet." And then her words tumbled out in a passion of communication, as though she hurried before her listener could be taken away. "I lived right in Salinas," she said. "Come there when I was a kid. Well, a show come through, an' I met one of the actors. He says I could go with that show.

But my ol' lady wouldn' let me. She says because I was on'y fifteen. But the guy says I coulda. If I'd went, I wouldn't be livin' like this, you bet."

Lennie stroked the pup back and forth. "We gonna have a little place—an' rabbits," he explained.

She went on with her story quickly, before she should be interrupted. " 'Nother time I met a guy, an' he was in pitchers. Went out to the Riverside Dance Palace with him. He says he was gonna put me in the movies. Says I was a natural. Soon's he got back to Hollywood he was gonna write to me about it." She looked closely at Lennie to see whether she was impressing him. "I never got that letter," she said. "I always thought my ol' lady stole it. Well, I wasn't gonna stay no place where I couldn't get nowhere or make something of myself, an' where they stole your letters. I ast her if she stole it, too, an' she says no. So I married Curley. Met him out to the Riverside Dance Palace that same night." She demanded, "You listenin'?"

"Me? Sure."

"Well, I ain't told this to nobody before. Maybe I ought'n to. I don' *like* Curley. He ain't a nice fella." And because she had confided in him, she moved closer to Lennie and sat beside him. "Coulda been in the movies, an' had nice clothes—all them nice clothes like they wear. An' I coulda sat in them big hotels, an' had pitchers took of me. When they had them previews I coulda went to them, an' spoke in the radio, an' it wouldn'ta cost me a cent because I was in the pitcher. An' all them nice clothes like they wear. Because this guy says I was a natural." She looked up at Lennie, and she made a small grand gesture with her arm and hand to show that she could act. The fingers trailed after her leading wrist, and her little finger stuck out grandly from the rest.

Lennie sighed deeply. From outside came the clang of a horseshoe on metal, and then a chorus of cheers. "Somebody made a ringer," said Curley's wife.

Now the light was lifting as the sun went down, and the sun streaks climbed up the wall and fell over the feeding racks and over the heads of the horses.

Lennie said, "Maybe if I took this pup out and throwed him away George wouldn't never know. An' then I could tend the rabbits without no trouble."

Curley's wife said angrily, "Don't you think of nothing but rabbits?"

"We gonna have a little place," Lennie explained patiently. "We gonna have a house an' a garden and a place for alfalfa, an' that alfalfa is for the rabbits, an' I take a sack and get it all fulla alfalfa and then I take it to the rabbits."

She asked, "What makes you so nuts about rabbits?"

Lennie had to think carefully before he could come to a conclusion. He moved cautiously close to her, until he was right against her. "I like to pet nice things. Once at a fair I seen some of them long-hair rabbits. An' they was nice, you bet. Sometimes I've even pet mice, but not when I could get nothing better."

Curley's wife moved away from him a little. "I think you're nuts," she said.

"No I ain't," Lennie explained earnestly. "George says I ain't. I like to pet nice things with my fingers, sof' things."

She was a little bit reassured. "Well, who don't?" she said. "Ever'body likes that. I like to feel silk an' velvet. Do you like to feel velvet?"

Lennie chuckled with pleasure. "You bet, by God," he cried happily. "An' I had some, too. A lady give me some, an' that lady was—my own Aunt Clara. She give it right to me—'bout this big a piece. I wisht I had that velvet right now." A frown came over his face. "I lost it," he said. "I ain't seen it for a long time."

Curley's wife laughed at him. "You're nuts," she said. "But you're a kinda nice fella. Jus' like a big baby. But a person can see kinda what you

156

mean. When I'm doin' my hair sometimes I jus' set an' stroke it 'cause it's so soft." To show how she did it, she ran her fingers over the top of her head. "Some people got kinda coarse hair," she said complacently. "Take Curley. His hair is jus' like wire. But mine is soft and fine. 'Course I brush it a lot. That makes it fine. Here—feel right here." She took Lennie's hand and put it on her head. "Feel right aroun' there an' see how soft it is."

Lennie's big fingers fell to stroking her hair.

"Don't you muss it up," she said.

Lennie said, "Oh! That's nice," and he stroked harder. "Oh, that's nice."

"Look out, now, you'll muss it." And then she cried angrily, "You stop it now, you'll mess it all up." She jerked her head sideways, and Lennie's fingers closed on her hair and hung on. "Let go," she cried. "You let go!"

Lennie was in a panic. His face was contorted. She screamed then, and Lennie's other hand closed over her mouth and nose. "Please don't," he begged. "Oh! Please don't do that. George'll be mad."

She struggled violently under his hands. Her feet battered on the hay and she writhed to be free; and from under Lennie's hand came a muffled screaming. Lennie began to cry with fright. "Oh! Please don't do none of that," he begged. "George gonna say I done a bad thing. He ain't gonna let me tend no rabbits." He moved his hand a little and her hoarse cry came out. Then Lennie grew angry. "Now don't," he said. "I don't want you to yell. You gonna get me in trouble jus' like George says you will. Now don't you do that." And she continued to struggle, and her eyes were wild with terror. He shook her then, and he was angry with her. "Don't you go yellin'," he said, and he shook her; and her body flopped like a fish. And then she was still, for Lennie had broken her neck.

He looked down at her, and carefully he removed his hand from over her mouth, and she lay still. "I don't want ta hurt you," he said, "but

George'll be mad if you yell." When she didn't answer nor move he bent closely over her. He lifted her arm and let it drop. For a moment he seemed bewildered. And then he whispered in fright, "I done a bad thing. I done another bad thing."

He pawed up the hay until it partly covered her.

From outside the barn came a cry of men and the double clang of shoes on metal. For the first time Lennie became conscious of the outside. He crouched down in the hay and listened. "I done a real bad thing," he said. "I shouldn't of did that. George'll be mad. An' .... he said .... an' hide in the brush till he come. He's gonna be mad. In the brush till he come. Tha's what he said." Lennie went back and looked at the dead girl. The puppy lay close to her. Lennie picked it up. "I'll throw him away," he said. "It's bad enough like it is." He put the pup under his coat, and he crept to the barn wall and peered out between the cracks, toward the horseshoe game. And then he crept around the end of the last manger and disappeared.

The sun streaks were high on the wall by now, and the light was growing soft in the barn. Curley's wife lay on her back, and she was half covered with hay.

It was very quiet in the barn, and the quiet of the afternoon was on the ranch. Even the clang of the pitched shoes, even the voices of the men in the game seemed to grow more quiet. The air in the barn was dusky in advance of the outside day. A pigeon flew in through the open hay door and circled and flew out again. Around the last stall came a shepherd bitch, lean and long, with heavy, hanging dugs. Halfway to the packing box where the puppies were she caught the dead scent of Curley's wife, and the hair arose along her spine. She whimpered and cringed to the packing box, and jumped in among the puppies.

Curley's wife lay with a half-covering of yellow hay. And the meanness and the plannings and the discontent and the ache for attention were all gone from her face. She was very pretty and simple, and her face was sweet and young. Now her rouged cheeks and her reddened lips made her seem alive and sleeping very lightly. The curls, tiny little sausages, were spread on the hay behind her head, and her lips were parted.

As happens sometimes, a moment settled and hovered and remained for much more than a moment. And sound stopped and movement stopped for much, much more than a moment.

Then gradually time awakened again and moved sluggishly on. The horses stamped on the other side of the feeding racks and the halter chains clinked. Outside, the mens' voices became louder and clearer.

From around the end of the last stall old Candy's voice came. "Lennie," he called. "Oh, Lennie! You in here? I been figuring some more. Tell you what we can do, Lennie." Old Candy appeared around the end of the last stall. "Oh,

Lennie!" he called again; and then he stopped, and his body stiffened. He rubbed his smooth wrist on his white stubble whiskers. "I di'n't know you was here," he said to Curley's wife.

When she didn't answer, he stepped nearer. "You oughten to sleep out here," he said disapprovingly; and then he was beside her and— "Oh, Jesus Christ!" He looked about helplessly, and he rubbed his beard. And then he jumped up and went quickly out of the barn.

But the barn was alive now. The horses stamped and snorted, and they chewed the straw of their bedding and they clashed the chains of their halters. In a moment Candy came back, and George was with him.

George said, "What was it you wanted to see me about?"

Candy pointed at Curley's wife. George stared. "What's the matter with her?" he asked. He stepped closer, and then he echoed Candy's words. "Oh, Jesus Christ!" He was down on his knees beside her. He put his hand over her heart. And finally, when he stood up, slowly and stiffly, his face was as hard and tight as wood, and his eyes were hard.

Candy said, "What done it?"

George looked coldly at him. "Ain't you got any idear?" he asked. And Candy was silent. "I should of knew," George said hopelessly. "I guess maybe way back in my head I did."

Candy asked, "What we gonna do now, George. What we gonna do now?"

George was a long time in answering. "Guess .... we gotta tell the .... guys. I guess we gotta get 'im an' lock 'im up. We can't let 'im get away. Why, the poor bastard'd starve." And he tried to reassure himself. "Maybe they'll lock 'im up an' be nice to 'im."

But Candy said excitedly, "We oughtta let 'im get away. You don't know that Curley. Curley gon'ta wanta get 'im lynched. Curley'll get 'im killed."

George watched Candy's lips. "Yeah," he said at last, "that's right, Curley will. An' the other

163

guys will." And he looked back at Curley's wife.

Now Candy spoke his greatest fear. "You an' me can get that little place, can't we, George? You an' me can go there an' live nice, can't we, George? Can't we?"

Before George answered, Candy dropped his head and looked down at the hay. He knew.

George said softly, "—I think I knowed from the very first. I think I knowed we'd never do her. He usta like to hear about it so much I got to thinking maybe we would."

"Then—it's all off?" Candy asked sulkily.

George didn't answer his question. George said, "I'll work my month an' I'll take my fifty bucks an' I'll stay all night in some lousy cat house. Or I'll set in some poolroom till ever'-body goes home. An' then I'll come back an' work another month an' I'll have fifty bucks more."

Candy said, "He's such a nice fella. I didn' think he'd do nothing like this."

164

George still stared at Curley's wife. "Lennie never done it in meanness," he said. "All the time he done bad things, but he never done one of 'em mean." He straightened up and looked back at Candy. "Now listen. We gotta tell the guys. They got to bring him in, I guess. They ain't no way out. Maybe they won't hurt 'im." He said sharply, "I ain't gonna let 'em hurt Lennie. Now you listen. The guys might think I was in on it. I'm gonna go in the bunk house. Then in a minute you come out and tell the guys about her, and I'll come along and make like I never seen her. Will you do that? So the guys won't think I was in on it?"

Candy said, "Sure, George. Sure I'll do that."

"O.K. Give me a couple minutes then, and you come runnin' out an' tell like you jus' found her. I'm going now." George turned and went quickly out of the barn.

Old Candy watched him go. He looked helplessly back at Curley's wife, and gradually his sorrow and his anger grew into words. "You

God damn tramp," he said viciously. "You done it, di'n't you? I s'pose you're glad. Ever'body knowed you'd mess things up. You wasn't no good. You ain't no good now, you lousy tart." He sniveled, and his voice shook. "I could of hoed in the garden and washed dishes for them guys." He paused, and then went on in a sing-song. And he repeated the old words: "If they was a circus or a baseball game . . . . we would of went to her . . . . jus' said 'ta hell with work,' an' went to her. Never ast nobody's say so. An' they'd of been a pig and chickens . . . . an' in the winter . . . . the little fat stove . . . . an' the rain comin' . . . . an' us jus' settin' there." His eyes blinded with tears and he turned and went weakly out of the barn, and he rubbed his bristly whiskers with his wrist stump.

Outside the noise of the game stopped. There was a rise of voices in question, a drum of running feet and the men burst into the barn. Slim and Carlson and young Whit and Curley, and Crooks keeping back out of attention range.

Candy came after them, and last of all came George. George had put on his blue denim coat and buttoned it, and his black hat was pulled down low over his eyes. The men raced around the last stall. Their eyes found Curley's wife in the gloom, they stopped and stood still and looked.

Then Slim went quietly over to her, and he felt her wrist. One lean finger touched her cheek, and then his hand went under her slightly twisted neck and his fingers explored her neck. When he stood up the men crowded near and the spell was broken.

Curley came suddenly to life. "I know who done it," he cried. "That big son-of-a-bitch done it. I know he done it. Why—ever'body else was out there playin' horseshoes." He worked himself into a fury. "I'm gonna get him. I'm going for my shot gun. I'll kill the big son-of-a-bitch myself. I'll shoot 'im in the guts. Come on, you guys." He ran furiously out of the barn. Carlson said, "I'll get my Luger," and he ran out too.

Slim turned quietly to George. "I guess Lennie done it, all right," he said. "Her neck's bust. Lennie coulda did that."

George didn't answer, but he nodded slowly. His hat was so far down on his forehead that his eyes were covered.

Slim went on, "Maybe like that time in Weed you was tellin' about."

Again George nodded.

Slim sighed. "Well, I guess we got to get him. Where you think he might of went?"

It semed to take George some time to free his words. "He—would of went south," he said. "We come from north so he would of went south."

"I guess we gotta get 'im," Slim repeated.

George stepped close. "Couldn' we maybe bring him in an' they'll lock him up? He's nuts, Slim. He never done this to be mean."

Slim nodded. "We might," he said. "If we could keep Curley in, we might. But Curley's gonna want to shoot 'im. Curley's still mad about his hand. An' s'pose they lock him up an' strap him down and put him in a cage. That ain't no good, George."

"I know," said George. "I know."

Carlson came running in. "The bastard's stole my Luger," he shouted. "It ain't in my bag." Curley followed him, and Curley carried a shotgun in his good hand. Curley was cold now.

"All right, you guys," he said. "The nigger's got a shotgun. You take it, Carlson. When you see 'um, don't give 'im no chance. Shoot for his guts. That'll double 'im over."

Whit said excitedly, "I ain't got a gun."

Curley said, "You go in Soledad an' get a cop. Get Al Wilts, he's deputy sheriff. Le's go now." He turned suspiciously on George. "You're comin' with us, fella."

"Yeah," said George. "I'll come. But listen, Curley. The poor bastard's nuts. Don't shoot 'im. He di'n't know what he was doin'."

"Don't shoot 'im?" Curley cried. "He got Carlson's Luger. 'Course we'll shoot 'im."

George said weakly, "Maybe Carlson lost his gun."

"I seen it this morning," said Carlson. "No, it's been took."

Slim stood looking down at Curley's wife. He said, "Curley—maybe you better stay here with your wife."

Curley's face reddened. "I'm goin'," he said. "I'm gonna shoot the guts outa that big bastard myself, even if I only got one hand. I'm gonna get 'im."

Slim turned to Candy. "You stay here with her then, Candy. The rest of us better get goin'."

They moved away. George stopped a moment beside Candy and they both looked down at the dead girl until Curley called, "You George! You stick with us so we don't think you had nothin' to do with this."

George moved slowly after them, and his feet dragged heavily.

And when they were gone, Candy squatted

down in the hay and watched the face of Curley's wife. "Poor bastard," he said softly.

The sound of the men grew fainter. The barn was darkening gradually and, in their stalls, the horses shifted their feet and rattled the halter chains. Old Candy lay down in the hay and covered his eyes with his arm.

6

THE deep green pool of the Salinas River was still in the late afternoon. Already the sun had left the valley to go climbing up the slopes of the Gabilan mountains, and the hilltops were rosy in the sun. But by the pool among the mottled sycamores, a pleasant shade had fallen.

A water snake glided smoothly up the pool, twisting its periscope head from side to side; and it swam the length of the pool and came to the legs of a motionless heron that stood in the shallows. A silent head and beak lanced down and plucked it out by the head, and the beak swallowed the little snake while its tail waved frantically.

A far rush of wind sounded and a gust drove through the tops of the trees like a wave. The sycamore leaves turned up their silver sides, the brown, dry leaves on the ground scudded a few feet. And row on row of tiny wind waves flowed up the pool's green surface.

As quickly as it had come, the wind died, and the clearing was quiet again. The heron stood in the shallows, motionless and waiting. Another little water snake swam up the pool, turning its periscope head from side to side.

Suddenly Lennie appeared out of the brush, and he came as silently as a creeping bear moves. The heron pounded the air with its wings, jacked itself clear of the water and flew off down river. The little snake slid in among the reeds at the pool's side.

Lennie came quietly to the pool's edge. He knelt down and drank, barely touching his lips to the water. When a little bird skittered over the dry leaves behind him, his head jerked up and he strained toward the sound with eyes and ears until he saw the bird, and then he dropped his head and drank again.

When he was finished, he sat down on the bank, with his side to the pool, so that he could watch the trail's entrance. He embraced his knees and laid his chin down on his knees.

The light climbed on out of the valley, and as it went, the tops of the mountains seemed to blaze with increasing brightness.

Lennie said softly, "I di'n't forget, you bet, God damn. Hide in the brush an' wait for George." He pulled his hat down low over his eyes. "George gonna give me hell," he said. "George gonna wish he was alone an' not have me botherin' him." He turned his head and looked at the bright mountain tops. "I can go right off there an' find a cave," he said. And he continued sadly, "—an' never have no ketchup— but I won't care. If George don't want me . . . . I'll go away. I'll go away."

And then from out of Lennie's head there came a little fat old woman. She wore thick bull's-eye glasses and she wore a huge gingham apron with pockets, and she was starched and clean. She stood in front of Lennie and put her hands on her hips, and she frowned disapprovingly at him.

And when she spoke, it was in Lennie's voice. "I tol' you an' tol' you," she said. "I tol' you, 'Min' George because he's such a nice fella an' good to you.' But you don't never take no care. You do bad things."

And Lennie answered her, "I tried, Aunt Clara, ma'am. I tried and tried. I couldn' help it."

"You never give a thought to George," she went on in Lennie's voice. "He been doin' nice things for you alla time. When he got a piece a pie you always got half or more'n half. An' if they was any ketchup, why he'd give it all to you."

"I know," said Lennie miserably. "I tried, Aunt Clara, ma'am. I tried and tried."

She interrupted him. "All the time he coulda had such a good time if it wasn't for you. He woulda took his pay an' raised hell in a whore house, and he coulda set in a pool room an' played snooker. But he got to take care of you."

Lennie moaned with grief. "I know, Aunt Clara, ma'am. I'll go right off in the hills an' I'll fin' a cave an' I'll live there so I won't be no more trouble to George."

"You jus' say that," she said sharply. "You're always sayin' that, an' you know sonofabitching well you ain't never gonna do it. You'll jus' stick around an' stew the b'Jesus outa George all the time."

Lennie said, "I might jus' as well go away. George ain't gonna let me tend no rabbits now."

Aunt Clara was gone, and from out of Lennie's head there came a gigantic rabbit. It sat on its haunches in front of him, and it waggled its ears and crinkled its nose at him. And it spoke in Lennie's voice too.

"Tend rabbits," it said scornfully. "You crazy bastard. You ain't fit to lick the boots of no rabbit. You'd forget 'em and let 'em go hungry. That's what you'd do. An' then what would George think?"

176

"I would *not* forget," Lennie said loudly.

"The hell you wouldn'," said the rabbit. "You ain't worth a greased jack-pin to ram you into hell. Christ knows George done ever'thing he could to jack you outa the sewer, but it don't do no good. If you think George gonna let you tend rabbits, you're even crazier'n usual. He ain't. He's gonna beat hell outa you with a stick, that's what he's gonna do."

Now Lennie retorted belligerently, "He ain't neither. George won't do nothing like that. I've knew George since—I forget when—and he ain't never raised his han' to me with a stick. He's nice to me. He ain't gonna be mean."

"Well, he's sick of you," said the rabbit. "He's gonna beat hell outa you an' then go away an' leave you."

"He won't," Lennie cried frantically. "He won't do nothing like that. I know George. Me an' him travels together."

But the rabbit repeated softly over and over, "He gonna leave you, ya crazy bastard. He gonna leave ya all alone. He gonna leave ya, crazy bastard."

Lennie put his hands over his ears. "He ain't, I tell ya he ain't." And he cried, "Oh! George —George—George!"

George came quietly out of the brush and the rabbit scuttled back into Lennie's brain.

George said quietly, "What the hell you yellin' about?"

Lennie got up on his knees. "You ain't gonna leave me, are ya, George? I know you ain't."

George came stiffly near and sat down beside him. "No."

"I knowed it," Lennie cried. "You ain't that kind."

George was silent.

Lennie said, "George."

"Yeah?"

"I done another bad thing."

"It don't make no difference," George said, and he fell silent again.

Only the topmost ridges were in the sun now.

The shadow in the valley was blue and soft. From the distance came the sound of men shouting to one another. George turned his head and listened to the shouts.

Lennie said, "George."

"Yeah?"

"Ain't you gonna give me hell?"

"Give ya hell?"

"Sure, like you always done before. Like, 'If I di'n't have you I'd take my fifty bucks——'"

"Jesus Christ, Lennie! You can't remember nothing that happens, but you remember ever' word I say."

"Well, ain't you gonna say it?"

George shook himself. He said woodenly, "If I was alone I could live so easy." His voice was monotonous, had no emphasis. "I could get a job an' not have no mess." He stopped.

"Go on," said Lennie. "An' when the enda the month come——"

"An' when the end of the month come I could take my fifty bucks an' go to a . . . . cat house . . . ." He stopped again.

Lennie looked eagerly at him. "Go on, George. Ain't you gonna give me no more hell?"

"No," said George.

"Well, I can go away," said Lennie. "I'll go right off in the hills an' find a cave if you don' want me."

George shook himself again. "No," he said. "I want you to stay with me here."

Lennie said craftily—"Tell me like you done before."

"Tell you what?"

" 'Bout the other guys an' about us.

George said, "Guys like us got no fambly. They make a little stake an' then they blow it in. They ain't got nobody in the worl' that gives a hoot in hell about 'em——"

"*But not us,*" Lennie cried happily. "Tell about us now."

George was quiet for a moment. "But not us," he said.

"Because——"

"Because I got you an'——"

"An' I got you. We got each other, that's what, that gives a hoot in hell about us," Lennie cried in triumph.

The little evening breeze blew over the clearing and the leaves rustled and the wind waves flowed up the green pool. And the shouts of men sounded again, this time much closer than before.

George took off his hat. He said shakily, "Take off your hat, Lennie. The air feels fine."

Lennie removed his hat dutifully and laid it on the ground in front of him. The shadow in the valley was bluer, and the evening came fast. On the wind the sound of crashing in the brush came to them.

Lennie said, "Tell how it's gonna be."

George had been listening to the distant sounds. For a moment he was business-like. "Look acrost the river, Lennie, an' I'll tell you so you can almost see it."

Lennie turned his head and looked off across

the pool and up the darkening slopes of the Gabilans. "We gonna get a little place," George began. He reached in his side pocket and brought out Carlson's Luger; he snapped off the safety, and the hand and gun lay on the ground behind Lennie's back. He looked at the back of Lennie's head, at the place where the spine and skull were joined.

A man's voice called from up the river, and another man answered.

"Go on," said Lennie.

George raised the gun and his hand shook, and he dropped his hand to the ground again.

"Go on," said Lennie. "How's it gonna be. We gonna get a little place."

"We'll have a cow," said George. "An' we'll have maybe a pig an' chickens . . . . an' down the flat we'll have a . . . . little piece alfalfa——"

"For the rabbits," Lennie shouted.

"For the rabbits," George repeated.

"And I get to tend the rabbits."

"An' you get to tend the rabbits."

Lennie giggled with happiness. "An' live on the fatta the lan'."

"Yes."

Lennie turned his head.

"No, Lennie. Look down there acrost the river, like you can almost see the place."

Lennie obeyed him. George looked down at the gun.

There were crashing footsteps in the brush now. George turned and looked toward them.

"Go on, George. When we gonna do it?"

"Gonna do it soon."

"Me an' you."

"You . . . . an' me. Ever'body gonna be nice to you. Ain't gonna be no more trouble. Nobody gonna hurt nobody nor steal from 'em."

Lennie said, "I thought you was mad at me, George."

"No," said George. "No, Lennie. I ain't mad. I never been mad, an' I ain't now. That's a thing I want ya to know."

The voices came close now. George raised the gun and listened to the voices.

Lennie begged, "Le's do it now. Le's get that place now."

"Sure, right now. I gotta. We gotta."

And George raised the gun and steadied it, and he brought the muzzle of it close to the back of Lennie's head. The hand shook violently, but his face set and his hand steadied. He pulled the trigger. The crash of the shot rolled up the hills and rolled down again. Lennie jarred, and then settled slowly forward to the sand, and he lay without quivering.

George shivered and looked at the gun, and then he threw it from him, back up on the bank, near the pile of old ashes.

The brush seemed filled with cries and with the sound of running feet. Slim's voice shouted, "George. Where you at, George?"

But George sat stiffly on the bank and looked at his right hand that had thrown the gun away. The group burst into the clearing, and Curley was ahead. He saw Lennie lying on the sand. "Got him, by God." He went over and looked down at Lennie, and then he looked back at George. "Right in the back of the head," he said softly.

Slim came directly to George and sat down beside him, sat very close to him. "Never you mind," said Slim. "A guy got to sometimes."

But Carlson was standing over George. "How'd you do it?" he asked.

"I just done it," George said tiredly.

"Did he have my gun?"

"Yeah. He had your gun."

"An' you got it away from him and you took it an' you killed him?"

"Yeah. Tha's how." George's voice was almost a whisper. He looked steadily at his right hand that had held the gun.

Slim twitched George's elbow. "Come on, George. Me an' you'll go in an' get a drink."

George let himself be helped to his feet. "Yeah, a drink."

Slim said, "You hadda, George. I swear you hadda. Come on with me." He led George into the entrance of the trail and up toward the highway.

Curley and Carlson looked after them. And Carlson said, "Now what the hell ya suppose is eatin' them two guys?"

THE END

JOHN STEINBECK was born in Salinas, California, on February 27, 1902. He studied marine biology at Stanford University and then traveled east on a freighter via the Panama Canal. Steinbeck went to New York to work as a newspaper reporter but soon returned to California and held a variety of jobs while he wrote. Steinbeck published *Tortilla Flat* in 1935 and *In Dubious Battle* in 1936 (both are available in The Modern Library), which established his reputation as a forceful writer. In 1939 he wrote *The Grapes of Wrath*, which summed up the despair of the early 1930's. John Steinbeck has also written short stories, books on sea life and other works of non-fiction. He was awarded the Nobel Prize for literature in 1962. He died in 1968.

MODERN LIBRARY GIANTS

A series of sturdily bound and handsomely printed, full-sized library editions of books formerly available only in expensive sets. These volumes contain from 600 to 1,400 pages each.

THE MODERN LIBRARY GIANTS REPRESENT A
SELECTION OF THE WORLD'S GREATEST BOOKS

MISCELLANEOUS